Candy Quilt Guilt

Miranda Hathaway Adventure #12

_____

Mary Devlin Lynch

and

Beth Devlin-Keune

© 2023 Mary Devlin Lynch/Beth Devlin-Keune
All rights reserved
Published by *DevlinsBooks*

ISBN 9798852021229

Dedication:
These last six months have been very challenging for me. This book is dedicated to those who defend you when you're not in the room. This book is dedicated to the heroes, the fighters, the loyal, the defenders.
To: Mary, Jean-Marie Lynch Cassidy, Dawn Devlin-Keune, and to my tribe led by Kim Toner-Swistock who reads every book, gets angry on my behalf, listens, and is just so kind.
This is not the end of your story, it's only a chapter.
Be kind to yourself.
Thank you, Beth

Contact Information:
E-mail: devlinsbooks@gmail.com
Facebook: devlinsbooks
Twitter: @devlinsbooks

One

The holiday season was over and the small town of Cutler was basking in the quiet of the early new year. The Christmas trees were stripped of their decorations and being composted down at the farm center. The glittering snowflake lights were removed from the street lamps and stored for next year. The empty gift boxes went to recycling; the leftover brightly patterned paper, gift tags and silky ribbons went to the attic.

The clean blanket of snow that covered Cutler every few days seemed to seal in the quiet of the town nestled between two mountains. There were, for sure, several months of cold and crisp weather still to come but most were turning their thoughts to Spring. Seed catalogs came in the mail, always a harbinger of hope, new sprouts, new beginnings.

Then Carl Baxter, the owner of Cutler's Candies, died suddenly and the town's well-being evaporated immediately into uncertainty and fear. Cutler's Candies was the town's biggest employer. A member of almost every Cutler family worked there and had for generations; it was a guaranteed paycheck, pension and benefits. No one could imagine a future for Cutler without the factory.

Perhaps his passing should not have been the surprise it appeared to be, the man was 85. Perhaps the townsfolk had just refused to anticipate what would happen when he passed. Could it jeopardize their very livelihoods and futures—and those of their children?

But before those questions could be addressed, he must be laid to his well-deserved rest. Mr. B, as he was called throughout the town, had a funeral that was standing-room only in the small church, the crowd subdued with somber faces and hats in hands. There was comfort in being surrounded by other families in the same boat as well as a need to pay respects.

His eldest son, Dennis, who looked like a younger version of his father with thinning light brown hair and green eyes behind round glasses, delivered a eulogy that captured the old man's spirit.

"Dad was a strong man," he said. "He ran the business with a firm hand and hard work. He taught us the value of a dollar but also the value of treating people decently and with respect."

Heads throughout the group nodded in sad agreement. His brother and sister sat silent in the front row, the sister wiping her eyes from time to time, other family filling the second row.

There was neither a graveside ceremony nor a wake. Word was that Mr. B wanted as little fuss as possible. Of course, everyone knew that the old guy was pretty tight with a buck in his personal affairs so he probably would have been rolling over in his grave if the whole town had been treated to the traditional free food and drink in his honor—and on his dime.

But despite his tendency to frugality, he had made sure that Cutler's Candies was well-maintained and safe, the aging factory kept up to code and following safety protocols to the letter. When a worker was injured, he had given them fair settlements (sometimes Carl even visited them). All the workers were paid a living wage and pensions when they were due. When a worker had an issue, he/she could walk right up the metal stairs inside the factory to the old man's office—and be heard.

The distressed faces in the pews reflected legitimate grief for the man's loss but also an urgent worry about the future of the candy factory. There were over a hundred jobs at stake for a town of about 3,500. The loss of these jobs would have a ripple effect that would hurt every single family in town in one way or another.

Sleepless nights followed. Everyone knew that the three children: Dennis, the oldest at 52, Clark the second son at 47, and Angela, 39, had differing opinions on what to do with the plant. While Mr. Baxter had kept the plant running, he refused to modernize or consider changes that would have kept it more competitive in the current market. Everyone knew that his offspring were frustrated by that.

Further rumors declared that its fate would depend upon Carl's will. CC was a family company and, as far as anyone knew, Carl's father had given his only son the company-lock, stock and barrel.

So had Carl done the same, giving it in full to his eldest son in the old world way of primogeniture? Or would Clark and Angela have talked him into splitting it three ways, having spent their entire adult lives working there?

The local Baxter attorney, Steve Montall, was fending off his own friends and family like a lottery winner as they tried to get answers about the contents of the will.

As head librarian at the Cutler Library and a member of Cutler Quilt Guild #1 as well as a lifelong resident of the town, I admit I thought about giving him a call.

While neither my husband nor I worked at the plant, the death of Mr. B hit us anyway.

John Bartlett, husband of Brittany, a member of our quilt guild, a friend, and mother of three children under seven, worked there. Where would he, with a high school education, find another job to support his family with insurance coverage and a pension?

Charley Boyer, husband of Sylvia, the proprietor of our best local diner and maker of the best meatloaf ever, had worked at the candy factory for over 40 years and was about to retire. What would happen to his pension? Suddenly, the entire future of our beloved little town seemed out of control.

We waited—and worried.

Two

Two days later, our Saturday meeting of the Cutler Quilt Guild #1 at Queenie's Quilt Shop reflected the town's subdued mood as we waited to see if Brittany would show up. She had to be beside herself wondering if John was going to lose his job. We chatted quietly as if a family member had died because that's how it felt.

We were all surprised when our brown-haired pixie bounded in in her usual high spirits.

"Geez, guys, who died?" She quipped when she saw our long faces. Then she caught herself. "Sorry. That might have been insensitive. RIP, Mr. B." She made a quick sign of the cross as she whipped off her puffy jacket, hat and gloves and tossed them onto the pile with the rest of ours on the cutting table.

We stared at her, then Sarah Moore, our oldest and gentlest quilter, said quietly, "It's the factory, hon."

Brittany's face fell but not for long. "There's just no point in fretting until we know." Her smile returned. "The will is being read on Monday. Sandy told me she's not gonna let the plant go under and I believe her. She'll make sure something good happens, wait and see."

We all nodded, comforted by her enthusiasm. Sandy Tressler, our mayor, was about the same age as Brit, early thirties, and one of the few in this town whose energy level matched that of Brittany herself.

She'd been bringing in new business and keeping the town clean as well as initiating a web site that kept everyone up to date of local goings on faster than the local newspaper. She was young, smart, and ambitious. It stood to reason that she would be all over this problem.

"Anything we can do…" I put out there and the rest of our trusty group echoed the sentiment.

"I know, thanks. Let's see what happens." She paused. "For now, just say a prayer." She rubbed her hands together. "Now let's do this!"

Part of the angst we had been feeling was not knowing what to do if the Baxters decided to sell. If they decided to sell out to Country Candies, the biggest candy maker in the state, there was no way for us to stop it but Country Candies had a reputation for putting profit first and employee retention somewhere further down the list of concerns. It was a commercial business with shareholders rather than a family-owned one and that made a big difference.

The door to Queenie's shop opened, the little bell merrily announcing the arrival of Polly Stanton, Millie Harticutt's niece and a sometimes member of our group. She wore bright red ear muffs and a long quilted coat. Her wavy brown hair was clean and shiny and pulled back into a high pony tail and she was smiling to show off her recent dental work. Neatly dressed in an oversized sweater and jeans, she was barely recognizable as the same messy and scowling woman who had practically slammed the door in my face when she first arrived.

Polly is part of our process for change in the guild. We have come to the conclusion that we have to figure out how to accept and integrate new members. It doesn't come easily when the rest of us have known each other practically from birth and the same quilters had formed the basic group for, well, ever.

Polly was a special case to me because when she first came to town, she wasn't very open and we weren't very welcoming. Frankly, Queenie and I thought she was a con artist because none of us ever knew Millie, whom she claimed to be her aunt, to have any family at all.

We truly believed she was trying to scam our elder friend to get at the Harticutt family home and fortune. Thankfully, we were wrong, so we decided the least we could do is let her join the guild whenever she wants as she makes a new life for herself here.

She almost always joins us for our monthly charity workshops which involve assembly line style of production and we can sure make use of the extra pair of hands.

Shelby Loggins is another sort of member of the guild. After Sarah Moore lost her twin sister Harriet in a terrible car accident almost two years ago, Sarah took Shelby under her wing. She had come up from the South and was staying uncomfortably with her aunt and uncle who run Danny's Donuts. Now she was sharing Sarah's big Victorian as she got her life together.

Shelby learned to quilt more as a matter of belonging in Cutler and for Sarah than interest. She works at the hair salon at the mall and is more interested in cosmetology than fabric. She comes with Sarah occasionally when she has a Saturday off, and we try to encourage her and make her welcome. Having a purpose and some support has made a dramatic change in that sullen, unkempt young woman, too. It would be hard to recognize her now with her lovely nails and well-done makeup, carrying herself with purpose and self-respect. She wasn't with us today.

No surprise to any of us that these two young women, both starting over, despite their age difference, have become friends. We are glad of it.

Our core group of five still anchor the guild and meet every week. My husband Gabe is also a bona fide member now. It felt a little odd at first having a man attend our meetings, I don't deny it, but it turned out his primary skill is running the long arm quilter, much to our delight. He helps Queenie with the projects usually backlogged by the rest of us who aren't so keen to learn it.

He doesn't make it every week now that he's found a second calling helping the Ryan family make custom birdhouses. He wasn't with me today which left the six of us.

Queenie McQueen, our president and fearless leader, who owns the very quilt shop in which we meet; Sarah Moore, our eldest quilter, a former teacher and an award winning hand quilter; Judy Smythin, who works part-time at the drug store and has a son in college and loves producing work for charity; Brit, our pixie mom who uses the guild as a chance to get out of the house and also makes lovely things for her little ones; me, Miranda Hathaway, town librarian and not particularly talented but enthusiastic quilter, and Polly.

So there we are and we have been quite content with this mini-family. But we have been made sadly aware by Harriet's death and a few other local events that nothing lasts forever. If the guild is to go on, we need to attract some more dedicated quilters. I know we all think about it and maybe the problem is that we need not only someone who loves the craft but someone we can all get along with as well (and, in all fairness, can get along with us)! I admit that, like the town, our little guild might have a problem with change.

In all fairness, we had added Nan Palmer, who had recently moved to town to live with her daughter. She wasn't a great quilter but her baked goods were to die for. She spent as much time off at baking competitions as she did in Cutler but we certainly enjoyed our breaks more when she showed up. This weekend, she was in Florida and who could blame her?

So we all took a breath and, with Polly's help, took on our charity task for the day.

"Happy New Year!" Queenie announced. "Today we are making pillowcases for the Pediatric Cancer Center. I had a call from a nurse there that a little extra cheer might be needed over there. I think we could all use a little pick me up right now too, so let's do this."

Queenie had chosen us to make pillowcases in our usual burrito method which required a 27" pattern for the body and a 9" piece for the cuff. She had piles of children's themed large pieces and brightly striped or single color cuff pieces.

As we always did, we tried to organize by speed and skill. Queenie of course was on her powder blue machine (matching all the walls in her shop and her logo bags), Judy and I taking the other two machines. We each picked our first set, then Brittany brought us more as we sewed. Polly pressed the finished cases and folded them neatly; Sarah kept the fabric flowing and attached our guild tag to each one with a small safety pin.

When it was time for break, we all went for the coffee and donuts Queenie had set out, talking about everything except the factory: the unusually balmy weather (in the 40s), family, vacations, good things. Then we went back to work, switching places. Brit took Judy's machine; Polly, for whom the straight stitching was no problem, took mine.

When Queenie called time, we had made 24 pillowcases which we declared a record.

"Woohoo!" Brittany crowed. "Happy New Year!"

Three

That "Happy New Year" echoed in my head on the way home. Even while I worried about the candy factory and the impact losing it might have, I had a lot to look forward to this year. It was mid-January; my daughter Zoey was due to give birth to triplets in early May. I was excited and terrified. I prayed for her safe delivery and for the health of the babies.

I made sure to sound encouraging and confident talking to my girl but my head was spinning, remembering what taking care of my one baby was like and wondering how on earth she and Michael were going to handle *three*. Every time she called, there seemed to be another major announcement.

Last week she told me they had decided to move. I tried to keep the screaming inside my head but her chuckle in response to my silence told me she heard it.

"I know, Mom, it's a lot, but seriously, how are we supposed to keep five people in a two-bedroom condo?"

That was a legitimate question but the timing was insane. How on earth could they pull this off with her looking like she'd swallowed three mini-basketballs and tired all the time? Because of the triplets and the need to keep the pregnancy going as long as possible toward the nine months, she had just started early maternity leave, for heaven's sake. My girl needed to rest.

"Okay." I said, accepting it but not thrilled.

"Oh damn, I have to pee again. Here's Michael."

"Hi, Mom." A deep voice said.

Yes, it tickled me that he had finally taken to calling me Mom. His own mother had been gone for some time now.

"Hi honey. Michael, how on earth are you going to pull this off?" I asked sternly. "You know that Zoey needs to rest."

He chuckled. "We're going to make it as easy as we can, I promise. We're looking at houses on line, working with an agent that a friend has recommended. Tomorrow, we're going to see three places and then decide. I'll handle the closing with the agent and then we'll hire a company to literally pack us up and move us. We don't have that much stuff really. Once we're in, we'll do some shopping on line and have stuff delivered. I promise you it's doable."

I breathed a sigh of relief but not much of one. I knew that the quick and easy steps he had laid out were fraught with possible issues. "Hmm, if you say so."

"I won't let anything happen to her—or the babies." He said in a quieter voice that choked me up.

"I know." I answered more kindly.

"Here she is, again."

"Did he tell you the plan, Mom? Easy peasy." Zoey said as if she didn't think I would hear the weariness in her voice.

"He did. And he promised me you would do as little as possible."

"Don't have much choice at this point. I can't see my feet and I have four months to go."

"When you're ready to move, would it help if I came for a visit?"

"I'd love that! Anytime actually, I'm home now all the time except for doctor's appointments. I could use the company." She sighed. "It's hard to be so awkward, Mom, I feel in my head like doing things my body has no interest in doing."

I chuckled. "I know, honey. I'll talk to Gabe and make a plan. Keep me posted on the house prospects."

"Will do. Love you, Mom."

"Love you too, my girl, and my grandbabies, too." I paused for effect. "Especially little Miranda."

She laughed, as I had intended. We didn't honestly know the sex of the babies but it had become a running joke as to what their names might be.

I caught up on a few small house chores. Then I checked the refrigerator and was relieved to see that we had leftover beef stew that I could just reheat and top off with a few biscuits.

When Gabe got home, we caught up on the day and he commiserated with me about the candy plant.

"It's all anyone wanted to talk about at the shop today."

"I know. It's a big cloud hanging over the town right now."

"You probably know Carl's children, right?"

Gabe was definitely getting used to Cutler, the kind of town where you know half the town and are related to the other half. "Sure, I went to school with Dennis, the oldest. He was a freshman when I was a senior. Clark was still in middle school. I didn't really know Angela, she's much younger. Dennis was the one who gave the eulogy at the funeral."

Gabe nodded. "So what happens now? Why is everyone so upset? The will hasn't even been read yet, right?"

"No, but the candy factory has been the major employer here forever. The company was started by Mr. Baxter's father, Joseph Baxter, back in the day. My goodness, they celebrated 100 years of production just last year. When Joe retired, Carl took over. He never wanted to retire, especially after his wife died, so he just kept running things. But the factory just hasn't been making the profits it used to." I paused. "From what I've heard, he didn't keep up with the times, didn't even want a website, you know, like that."

"That's interesting. Do you know what happens now that he's passed?"

I shrugged. "That's what's driving everybody crazy. The story has always been that the company was fully owned by the family. I'm not even sure there's stock or anything. I thought Carl owned it outright and the children just worked there. It could go entirely to Dennis as the oldest son the same way."

"Isn't that a recipe for disaster, now," he said thoughtfully. "If I had been Carl, I'd have been watching my back." He paused. "I wouldn't want to be Dennis, either."

I chuckled. "Oh come on now, you're being overly dramatic. Carl died of natural causes because he was 85. No foul play. This is Cutler, remember?"

14

I really did accept that Carl had died of natural causes but that didn't answer any questions. What if he had left it to all three of them and they disagreed on the future of the factory?

Harry, our rather hefty gray and white cat with beautiful green eyes, meandered through in time to hear the end of the conversation so we included him as we often do.

We phrase our questions carefully because if more than a 'yes' or 'no' answer is involved, you can get an earful of catspeak that simply does not translate.

I picked him up and looked into his green cat eyes. "Harry, is everything gonna be okay down at the candy factory?"

He narrowed his eyes, then wiggled to get down. We all know that means he doesn't want to answer.

I held him firmly. "Come on. We need an answer."

He mumbled a bit, then looked right at me. "Neeoooowww."

I put him down quickly, he's no lightweight.

Gabe frowned. "Well, damn."

I turned my worried face to my husband. "But what does that mean? Does it mean the factory will close? If Dennis takes over, will he sell it to Country Candies? Do his brother and sister have a say? And will our people lose their jobs?"

Gabe clapped a hand to his forehead. "Harry doesn't want to talk about it and I don't either, not right now." He massaged my shoulders lightly with his big hands. "I'm hungry. How about some supper before we solve the problems of the world, or the mini-world of Cutler at least?"

15

It was Saturday night so we rented a movie. I chose a comedy because I needed a good laugh (Melissa McCarthy always does the trick).

Then to top off my calming end of the day ritual, I went into the seldom used dining room and looked at The Dollhouse Quilt which Millie Harticutt had given me herself, hanging in pride of place on the wall. I swear, I see something different every time I look at it. It's an amazing piece of work, a complete replica of the Harticutt home, complete with the special room that holds the family quilts and the antique furniture and rugs and, well, everything. It's not just a quilt but a work of art and I know it deserves to be where more people can see it.

It had been displayed at Queenie's Quilt Shop for a few weeks and drawn visitors from all over. She only let it go when she decided the traffic was more than she needed.

But then it was given to me. Seeing it calms me down much like working on my own quilting projects does. I know I need to share it but I may not be quite ready to let it go. Displaying it at the library occasionally is as far as I've gotten in loosening my grip. Sometimes I feel selfish but I seem to be okay with that, for now. I think, and hope, I'll know when it's time to let it go.

Four

Sunday passed with a slow parade of phone calls and text messages about the factory. To get away from all that, Gabe and I finally left town, leaving our phones behind, and drove over to the buffet in Lewiston. We don't do it often because who really needs 'all you can eat' on a regular basis?

But it is fun to put a few bites of this and that on one plate and then use another one to sample their desserts. Personally, I get a little giddy when I have a brownie, bread pudding, an apple dumpling, and vanilla ice cream all on one plate. After stuffing ourselves, we drove around for a while, enjoying the countryside and the quiet before we went home.

We played a taped Jeopardy game with Harry since we'd missed a few this past week. He sits in his recliner (yes, he has his own) between Gabe and me and makes his cat answers for which he gets full credit. It sounds unusual, I know, but he insists on being a full-fledged member of the family and has since he walked in the back door and made himself at home. I was on a roll myself and beat Gabe which is a rare occurrence, thanks to the inclusion of a Bibliotheca category.

I was as relaxed as I've been for a few days and slept better too until my alarm went off.

Oversized coffee in hand, I arrived at my desk ready to face my inbox. My assistant librarian, Lucy Huntley, is fully up to the task of covering Saturdays but my inbox does have more paper in it Monday than it does when I leave on Friday. I can't claim that it's often empty but it's not usually overflowing either.

I texted Dee, my BFF since we were six, and made a date for noon at Sylvia's and got down to work. She didn't even ask what was going on; she knew, just like everyone else.

Lucy and I worked our way through the mail and the bank deposit and she told me how the weekend author events had gone. Our little library serves as a social hub, given the limited facilities in town. So there had been a senior social hour Friday night and a local mystery writer had drawn a crowd on Saturday.

We had recently started closing on Sundays and no one seemed to mind so far. Cutler is still a town where a lot of folks spend Sunday in church and having dinner with the family. The number of users simply didn't justify keeping it open. This time of year, especially, we have to be mindful of our budget; heat and electricity don't come cheap.

The wind was up and I hurried down the street to Sylvia's, keeping my head down. It was with relief that I closed the door securely behind me. I slid into the booth and Sylvia waved at me from behind the counter. I raised two fingers and she nodded her understanding that I wanted two hot chocolates, our regular cold weather drink order. (Our summer drink is iced tea, of course.}

Dee hurried in and wiggled into the booth, a little out of breath and looking cranky.

"Is everything okay?" I asked.

She shrugged out of her coat. "It's this damned factory business. Even the kids are upset and I'm having a time getting them to focus on English Lit when half their fathers or mothers might be out of work anytime." She sighed. "A couple of them were counting on getting jobs there themselves after they graduate."

"Oh Lord, I hadn't thought about that." I shook my head. "We need to know, good or bad, don't we?"

Sylvia put our drinks down and, for the first time in, well, years, she didn't throw a snarky comment at Dee. She delighted in getting Dee's dander up and I rather enjoyed her witty repartee. Somehow, Dee never seemed to appreciate it or to find a way to ignore it. I always thought maybe Sylvia worked on her quips and had one ready when we showed up. It was a game that never seemed to get old—until now.

"Today's specials are ham pot pie or a meatball sub with homemade chips." Sylvia stood quietly and waited.

Dee and I looked at each other.

"The pot pie, please," I said in a subdued voice.

"Me too." Dee added, "Thanks."

Sylvia nodded and went back into the kitchen.

"It's the end of the world as we know it," I whispered to Dee, trying to lighten the mood.

Dee simply nodded. I swear she looked disappointed, too.

We sipped our hot chocolate until Sylvia put the plates in front of us and the check on the edge of the table without saying a word. Then she went to take another order.

19

As soon as I was fairly sure she couldn't hear us, I whispered to Dee, "Charley."

She nodded. "I know."

Sylvia's husband Charley had put in over 40 years at the candy factory and was about to retire. They were counting on his pension. We knew they had been making plans to buy an RV and start taking actual vacations.

"So when is the will being read?"

"Today at 3," She whispered back. "A couple of local fools are taking bets."

"What?"

"I know. But the money's on the factory closing."

"Oh no. Have you heard anything?"

"Not a word. Steve and Paula went out of town for the weekend because they just couldn't take it."

"I hear that. It's been awful." I managed a smile. "I almost called him myself."

"You'd be the only one in town who didn't. I'll call you soon as I hear anything."

I patted her hand. "Likewise."

We ate quickly and went back to work.

I was a little surprised. If Dee, who has ears to the ground all over town, hadn't heard anything about the will yet, there was nothing to hear.

Five

The whole town was holding its breath. Even the Library felt quieter than usual and it's always pretty quiet. Giving up any pretext of getting work done, Lucy sat down in front of my desk just before 4 o'clock and we both stared at the phone.

"Hello?" I said tentatively when it rang.

"It's me. Listen, the word is out. The old man left the factory in three shares to the kids BUT with the proviso that they can't sell it! He split his money between them as well. Believe it or not, he had about $12 mil in the bank. That's it for now."

Dee clicked off before I could react. I wasn't surprised. She had a lot of calls to make.

I smiled at Lucy. "The factory goes to all three and they can't sell it."

A sigh of relief escaped her lips but then the frown came back. "That doesn't actually mean they have to keep it open though, does it?"

"Well, that was a short-lived moment of relief. Thanks."

She chuckled. "Could be worse."

I shrugged. "True."

She went back to her office and I called Gabe. There was no point pretending that I was going to get any work done in this last hour.

"Hi, honey."

"You heard."

"I did."

"But…"

"Exactly."

There was a moment of silence. "Hold on a sec." He put me on hold. It didn't happen often so I knew something important was going on. I waited.

"Miranda? Another flash just came in. A customer told BJ that the daughter is packing her bags and leaving town."

"She wanted to sell."

"That's the word."

I actually chuckled. "It does tickle me that you got this news before me."

He laughed appreciatively. "At last, I feel like a local."

"Don't get a big head. I'll see you at home."

"Yep. I should be there about 5:30 or so. Do you want to go out?"

I gave it a thought. "Honestly, a pizza would do me. I feel like there's already a lot to digest."

"Got you. I'll bring it with me."

"Gabe," I said gratefully. "I love you."

There was the slightest pause. I have tried to say those words more often but the fact is that I don't say them to him as often as he says them to me. My first husband, Harry, was a Marine and he demonstrated his love for me and Zoey in a lot of ways that were, well, non-verbal. But Gabe was different. His first marriage hadn't worked out too well and I often felt he was determined to make the most of the second chance we had both been given. I appreciate that.

"I love you too, beautiful."

To my surprise, the phone rang again. It was Queenie.

"Hey, Miranda. You heard?"

"Yeah, but I'm not sure what it means."

"I know. We still have to wait and see. But that's not why I called." She took a breath. "You know how we keep talking about bringing in new quilters but never actually do anything about it?"

"Sure."

"So I had a thought. What if we offer a free quilting lesson at the shop? Maybe there are some locals who sew but are afraid to quilt who would come in."

I gave it no more than a moment's thought. "Wow, that's a great idea. Why..."

She laughed. "Why didn't we think of this before? No idea."

"I'm in. And it gives us a chance to..."

"Look them over and see if we want them in guild."

I laughed out loud. "We sound like an old married couple. Stop finishing my..."

"SENTENCES." Queenie bellowed through the phone.

I clicked off.

She texted me. "Get back to you with date..."

"And time!" I texted back.

I love that woman. It was nice to be reminded that life would go on, no matter what happened to the candy factory.

Six

"We understand the importance of Cutler's Candies to this community. Don't forget, we grew up here too. As you probably all know, our father's will decreed that it could not be sold. However, we may need to pivot the factory in some way to ensure that it remains viable. But, for now, we have no intention of closing it. Salaries will be paid, insurance will be paid, and pensions will be paid. We anticipate returning to production next week."

As soon as Dennis Baxter released that statement, phones lit up and the town web site trumpeted the news the next morning: CUTLER'S CANDIES TO REMAIN OPEN!

Dennis and Clark met with Sandy and there was more detail to that discussion. But the headline was enough to let most of the town exhale even while Sandy and the brothers continued to think about long-term solutions.

When asked about his sister, Clark smiled and said, off the record, that it was actually easier to deal with the situation without Angela. She had signed a power of attorney giving either of her brothers the ability to make decisions for her. She was happy to head off to the City to start a new life.

The entire town went to bed that night feeling relieved and hopeful.

BOOM! I sat straight up. Had I dreamt that sound? My heart was racing. I looked over at Gabe to see if he was awake, too but he was already out of bed and getting dressed. I remembered to exhale. Not a dream.

"Gabe?"

"Sounded like an explosion."

He was out the door while I was still trying to understand what had happened. Sirens and horns filled the night; voices and running feet followed.

Gabe sent a four word text: IT'S THE CANDY FACTORY.

I made coffee and sat at the kitchen table, texting with my friends around town. They sent me pictures of the aftermath of the explosion.

Red-orange flames had burst through the roof and the clear night sky was dimmed by soot and dust. Pieces of metal, wood and bricks had flown in every direction until odd piles were spaced around the building and into the parking lot.

It was about 5AM when Gabe came back, dirty and smelling of smoke. I hugged him tightly, then pulled back and looked him over carefully looking him over for any injuries.

"I'm fine, honey," he said hoarsely.

"How bad?" I whispered.

"I'd say about half the building."

Tears filled my eyes. "But why?"

My husband sighed. "Good question."

"Was anyone hurt?"

He looked away.

"Oh Gabe." I held my breath once again. Which one of our many friends and family had been hurt in the explosion?

"Night watchman, Fred Smith, knocked unconscious, burns. He's at the hospital."

"Will he, is he…"

Gabe shook his head. "Doesn't look good."

Harry was suddenly there, wrapping himself around our ankles until Gabe picked him up and included him in our comforting hug.

He let out a stream of sorrowful Catish as if he was mourning a loss. No translation needed.

Seven

Gabe went back to bed and I made my way early down to the edge of town where the candy factory sat next to Sunny Spring.

There was only grayness everywhere. The overcast sky with its snow-laden clouds melded with the smoking ashes and black/gray shards. And there was silence, an odd empty silence.

Behind the piles of debris, you could see straight through the plant to mangled machinery.

I was not alone in my need to see for myself so that I could believe. Shortly, Dee and Judy joined me and about 30 other people who had come down to view the wreckage. Huddled in our winter gear, our breath visible in the morning chill, we simply stood and stared. The smarter amongst us held steaming coffees.

We spoke in hushed voices—as if it mattered.

Dee said quietly, "Fred didn't make it."

My throat thickened. "My God, I thought he had retired already. He must have been over 80."

Judy nodded. "Yep. After his wife died, he stayed on. It's not like it was hard duty. He had a little shed by the door with a chair and once or twice a night he made the rounds of the plant with a flashlight."

27

Dee added. "Everybody knew that. It's not like anything was ever going to happen, right?"

"But it did. So all anyone had to do was see if Fred was in his chair, most likely napping." She met my eyes and then we both looked to the side of the building where Fred would have been sitting in his chair inside his heated little booth. Fred's security booth was glass from about waist high. He'd have had a light on inside to signal that he was on duty. Yes, it would have been easy to see him.

"So it was an accident, right?" I said.

"I'm sure as hell going to find out." A deep male voice came from behind me. I turned to find Jimmy Haynes, our chief of police, standing there, his eyes red and his face unshaven.

He wasn't yet thirty, our Chief, and he had stepped into a job that used to be mostly about parking tickets and Saturday night fights but in recent years had included drugs, murder, and now he might be adding arson.

We all turned toward the sound of weeping and saw Melody Hutchins, Fred Smith's daughter, barely standing with her daughter Heather's arm around her.

Heather was trying to get her mother to leave.

"I have to see. I have to see." Melody sobbed.

Judy moved over to help support Melody and we heard voices counselling her to leave, go home and rest. She had been in our class at school; her Heather had been in school with Zoey. There are few strangers in this town.

After a few more minutes of helpless watching, I went to work. Like everyone else there, I didn't know what else to do.

Lucy arrived, gave me a subdued nod, and went quietly to her desk. The library was open but there was no one coming in. While there were only a few folks in town who could actually help in any way, it felt somehow unseemly, I think, for the rest to go about their usual business, somehow disrespectful to Fred.

I cleared the top of my inbox and then went over to Lucy.

She clicked off her phone, tears in her eyes. Then her shoulders fell. "Why, Miranda, why?"

I shook my head. "I have no idea, honey."

"But you'll try to find out, right?" She added, "I love Jimmy, you know that, but this is just more than he signed up for. You and Gabe will help him, won't you?" She twisted the diamond engagement ring on her finger. She and Jimmy had been together several years now and were waiting for a good time to plan their wedding.

The truth was that I hadn't thought this through to finding out who had done this to our town or why. Maybe I was numb or maybe I didn't want to. I didn't know what to say to Lucy's anxious face so I said what she wanted to hear. "Of course we will."

The library was empty so we closed early and sent Grace, who had been sitting at the front desk with her handkerchief in hand, home.

When I got home, I took a nap. Gabe came in just as I was getting up an hour later.

"Any news?" I asked at once.

"The Fire Marshall is there; the insurance investigators have been in touch. The first question is whether it was an accident or arson." Then he added, "Let's face it, their Dad said the Baxters couldn't sell, he didn't say they couldn't burn the place down."

Gabe had already decided not to mention the even more obvious—to anyone. If it was arson, Fred Smith was the only one there at the time. Gabe and the chief had agreed not to say it out loud for now. There was enough sadness and distress without blackening the name of the old guy until the reports came in to show that it was necessary.

"You will help Jimmy, won't you? Lucy's awfully worried." I pleaded.

"Of course." He managed a smile. "I'm still an auxiliary deputy; all hands to the pump."

I had been almost listening to the answer I knew I could count on but, my duty to Lucy done, my thoughts were wandering back to what Gabe had said.

Now I was frowning. "So you're saying that the Baxter boys threw out that happy picture of keeping the place open as a smokescreen, intending to get rid of it once and for all."

"Something like that."

"Good Lord. What an awful thing to do." I crossed my arms. "I don't believe it."

"Money is a strong motivator." He shrugged. "It's a lot more work for them to keep it going than it is to get rid of it and sell the land. Along with the $4 million each in cash they got, they'll be set for life without lifting a finger."

I opened my mouth but he shook his head.

"I know, sweetheart, it's Cutler. They're Cutler born and bred. I'm sorry, honey, but that doesn't mean they will always put the town first."

I felt my chin go up. *But it does.* I said to myself. *Yes, it does.*

Eight

Father O'Shea had a dilemma. He had information that might, just might, be relevant to the investigation into the candy factory fire. But it had been given to him under seal of confession, and that seal remained even when the penitent was gone. He had called the Bishop and asked for guidance, in the broadest terms of course, and the answer came back the same.

He prayed for guidance from above too but the only voice he heard told him he needed to find a way to get the information to Jimmy Haynes. He honestly believed that the penitent who had shared his crimes with his priest would have understood.

In all his years in Cutler, no one had ever confessed anything that he believed he could not hold secret. If a man confessed to drinking, stealing, abusing, Father O'Shea found a way to get the penitent to make it right. One way or another, the drinkers landed in the cells, the thieves got caught, the abusers, well sometimes justice took things into its own hands. He'd had one man who abused his wife and child get run over by a tractor (accidentally) on the farm. These truths were not his to tell and he might have kept watch for the outcome but he never violated his oath.

But this was different. As far as he knew he was the only one carrying the secret. The penitent was dead. It was likely that his family didn't know. Yes, Father O'Shea had a problem. He was considering writing an anonymous note to the police chief. He opened his computer and put his hands on the keys. He froze and then his eyes filled and he couldn't see. He heard from the conscience that spoke to him. *Wait.*

Melody Hutchins was experiencing a similar dilemma. As she was cleaning her father's room, she had found an envelope under the mattress. Her father had never had that much money at one time in his whole life. She knew that for certain. He had cashed his paycheck from the factory and given most of it to her to help with the bills.

There was a note. She sat on the edge of the bed and wept.

Dear Melody, I never had much so ther ain't much to leave. But I done wrong and I need to own it before I go. Them accidents at the factry, that was me. Some foks paid me good mony to do it. I seen to it that not much harm was done. The factry ain't gonna last after the old man goes anyways. I aint goin to say who it was the blame is mine. I kno it was wrong, but I had no mony to even pay for my funral. So now you do. Love, Dad

She cried some more, then she washed her face, composed herself as best she could, and went to speak to her priest.

When Father O'Shea heard his secretary/housekeeper speaking to someone outside his door, he ran a hand through his short silver hair, took a breath, and opened the door.

Melody Hutchins gave him a timid smile as he waved her into the chair in front of his desk.

Was she here to answer his prayers? Or was she here as tests of his ability to hold back the words that were choking him?

Without a word, she pulled a crumpled note from her bag and handed it to him. Then she pulled out a handful of tissues and wiped her eyes and blew her nose, then looked at him for the first time.

"You're not surprised." She nodded. "Dad confessed, didn't he? I'm so glad. He doesn't deserve hell, Father, he doesn't," she added vehemently.

He put the note down and sighed. "That is not for me to judge, Melody. Now, how can I help *you*?"

She took a deep breath. "If I give this note to Jimmy, the whole town will know what Dad did. His whole life, his service in the army, his work with the veterans, the way he took care of Mom all those years, it will all mean nothing. He'll be the man who blew up the factory. He'll be the man who put everyone out of work."

The priest looked at her with understanding and compassion. "We don't know who actually caused the explosion. In this note, your father only admits to small acts of disruption—mischief."

She closed her eyes for a second. "It doesn't matter. They'll decide it was him and, even if that changes later, the damage to my family will be done. You know that as well as I do. Dad will be the headline now and by the time they find out who did the explosion, it will be a footnote." She added softly, "He didn't do it. You know he didn't."

He did. He offered her a cup of coffee and made them each one. They sipped the hot liquid in silence for a few minutes. Then he put his cup down.

"My dear Melody, you came here already knowing what you have to do." He looked at her and smiled gently. "I can come with you if you like."

She put down her cup on the edge of the desk. "Yes, I know what to do. It just felt good to talk to someone first." She sighed. "Someone who wouldn't give me the look I'm going to get from everyone I pass on the street from now on." She stood up. "You don't need to come, Father, I'll go over to the station right now."

He came around the desk and laid a hand on her shoulder. "May God give you strength and courage."

Tears filled her eyes; she nodded. "Thank you."

When the door closed behind her, he sank into his chair and closed his own eyes, asking God to forgive him for the relief he felt at this burden being lifted off his shoulders. Then he said a prayer for Melody and her family and wished there was more he could do.

Then he realized there was, of course. She would be back, asking him to hold the funeral mass. He took a breath and smiled. That he could do.

Nine

Jimmy Haynes was staring at the preliminary Fire Marshall's notes on his computer, organizing his investigation into the factory explosion, when Trixie, the front desk receptionist, stuck her head into his office.

"Sorry to interrupt, chief, but Melody Hutchins is here."

He placed the papers that were on his desk face down, closed the screen, and stood as the pale woman stepped inside, clutching her purse.

It was not a time for smiles or casual greetings even though he'd known her all his life. His mother worked with her at the hospital. Her face was sad and set. She had come here to tell him something and he needed to listen.

"I'm so sorry for your loss, Mrs. Hutchins." He said gently. "Come in and take a seat. What can I do for you?"

Tears ran silently down her cheeks but she raised her chin in determination. "I have information." Her voice was broken and dry.

He stood and got her a glass of water from the small tank on the side table. She took it and gulped it down in one go but shook her head when he offered a refill. She sank into the chair, opened her purse, and handed him the note.

He read it quickly, laid it on the desk, and rubbed a hand across his stubbly face. "Ah damn."

It was as if he had forgotten she was there until he looked up and saw the anguish on her face. "I'm sorry."

She nodded and swallowed. "Me, too."

"This doesn't mean..."

"I know, Jim. But we both know what it means in a town this size. Dad will be villainized by the end of the day." She cleared her throat. "That can't be helped. Now I need to know from you if I can use this money to pay for his funeral like he asked." She swallowed. "He was right to say we don't have the extra."

He knew that and he knew why. Her mother had died from cancer but it had taken years, long years of all the care her family could give her that left them with crushing debt. He knew lots of folks who had managed to help out without insulting the family or damaging their pride. But doing the right thing had come with a hefty price and they were still paying. Then Melody's husband had been killed in a car crash a year ago and the small insurance payout had barely covered his funeral expenses.

He leaned back in his chair which squeaked in protest and drummed his fingers on the edge of the desk. The note was a confession to a crime, or series of crimes, and the money was clearly payment for the commission of those crimes. He wished she hadn't asked. He wished he'd never seen it.

His mind raced. These small crimes had likely nothing to do with the arson that had cost Fred his life. Jimmy also knew what would happen to this recovered money. He had asked once before out of curiosity in another case. It went to the Asset Recovery Department in Harrisburg where half a dozen sets of paperwork later, it would either go into the state general fund or possibly be sent to some police department as additional funding. For this, Fred's reputation should go down the drain?

A small voice interrupted his train of thought. "He didn't do it."

His training told him that Fred should be his first suspect; he was, after all, the only person they knew to be on scene at the time. He and Gabe had already discussed that. Even his daughter had figured it out. His gut told him Fred had not started that fire. If he was wrong and could prove it, well, he would. But not now.

He found his official police voice. "If this money should prove to be related to the current crime of arson or the involuntary manslaughter under investigation, I will have to impound the money since it was received as payment for the commission of a related crime."

He lowered his voice. "In the meantime, this note is going to disappear for now."

Melody's eyes widened. "What?"

He nodded. "I never saw it and neither did you. You are going to tell anyone who asks that Fred must have been hoarding money under his mattress all these years to pay for his funeral." His eyes bored into hers. "Got it?"

She took a breath and nodded. "I got it."

"You will tell no one, and I mean no one, anything about this."

"Someone already knows."

Jimmy's heart sank. The town grapevine would already be humming. "Who?"

"Father O'Shea."

He released his breath and smiled. "That's okay then."

Melody managed a smile. "Yes," she said with relief.

She wiped her eyes one last time as she stood. "I'm gonna go right on over to the funeral home."

He looked down at his desk. "Can't stop you."

She took hold of the door knob and opened it. Without looking back, he heard her say, "Thanks, Jimmy."

When she was gone, he sat there for a few minutes. He was skirting the edges of the law and he knew it. But Fred Smith was a Cutler man his whole life, a good man, and he might have given his life to give his daughter money for his funeral.

It might not have been the strictly legal thing to let Fred have his funeral but Jimmy knew he would be able to live with that easier than the alternative. If he had taken that money and entered it into evidence with the note, the whole town would have known…before the funeral. He shook his head. Nope.

The fact was that the note did not prove that Fred had anything to do with the fire. He might have been guilty of nothing worse than criminal mischief. The previous incidents had been those of setting off the sprinklers and drenching the place, a melted breaker box, some broken windows, and the like. No permanent harm done.

It was possible that whoever had hired Fred to mess up the workings of the factory had taken it a big step further after Carl died. Fred might have refused to do their dirty work so if he got in the way that was too bad. It sounded plausible.

He could see Fred startled awake in his booth by a sound he wasn't used to hearing so he roused himself and started to walk toward the noise. The blast blew him straight back to the floor as the flames rushed toward him. Even in his head, it was hard to envision the old man lying there, burned and broken, waiting for the help that came too late.

Jimmy was going to wait until the insurance reports came in and maybe until after the funeral. His priority was finding out who did this to his town and to Fred Smith, whom he saw as collateral damage, and, until every shred of evidence had been exhausted, not a suspect.

Ten

Rumors were flying through the air in Cutler as fast everyone's phones could ping with updates. Grace reported that Dennis's wife, Jasmine, was overheard saying she suspected Angela of being involved! Could you imagine? And yet, Nancy Morgan, who had been the old man's right hand for over 50 years, had finally admitted that there had been fights, loud and vicious, in the past year, and that Angela was usually involved.

Dee and I traded info over lunch on Monday at Jessie's Grill, a new small café that had opened on a side street to avoid Sylvia's, just for now, unable to face Sylvia's worried expression.

We placed our order and then, after our drinks came, I opened, keeping my voice down.

"I've heard that some folks think Angela was involved."

Dee nodded. "I'm hearing the same thing. But I find it hard to believe she could do such a thing." She leaned forward. "There is another set of rumors going around, though. Remember all those weird accidents that have been happening? Like when the sprinklers went off?"

I nodded. Everyone had heard about that. "Sure. It seemed like a short in the system or something. It didn't do more than wet things down for a shift."

"Right." She lowered her voice even further. "I'm hearing it was Fred Smith himself who caused those accidents."

I actually gasped. "What? Get out. That's absurd. Why would that sweet old man do such a thing?"

Dee rubbed her fingers together. "Money. According to Bonnie McMurray who works at the funeral home, he's having a real nice send off." She shrugged. "We both know Melody doesn't have that kind of money."

"Maybe he had insurance."

Dee shot me a look with a snort. "Fred couldn't spell insurance, let's be real."

"But if the money was a payoff for causing those accidents, wouldn't Jimmy have to, like, impound it?"

Dee nodded. "Maybe. He might be playing dumb for Melody's sake. Or he might not be playing..." She stopped herself. "I'm sure he's doing the best he can."

"Lord, I'm glad I'm not Jimmy right now."

The young blonde proprietor put two turkey clubs with chips and pickle on the side in front of us, smiled, and left.

"I know, right?" Dee was saying. She took a break to try to stuff the thick sandwich in her mouth and then waved her pickle in my direction. "Betcha he'll be calling in the staties. Word from the station is that Dick Dixon is going to say officially that this was no accident."

I swallowed a big bite and nodded. "But I have to believe there was no intention to hurt anyone, don't you think? I'm guessing they thought old Fred would be asleep in his chair outside. He probably was, then heard a noise and went to see."

Dee stopped her sandwich halfway to her mouth and sighed. "Once you're over 80, you should be allowed to die in your sleep."

"Amen."

We ate most of our lunch in sad silence.

Eleven

The next morning, Dick Dixon, the town's fire marshal, took the seat in front of Jimmy's desk, setting a solid tote on the floor beside him.

"'Mornin, Jim."

"Dick."

The older man cleared his throat. "This here's a tricky one and I'm sure glad I'm not you."

That actually brought a smile to Jimmy's haggard face. "Seems like I've been hearing that a lot lately."

Dick nodded. "So here's what I think happened and my secretary is writing it up all formal for you." He drew a breath. "That 100-year blanket thing that was hanging in Carl's office after it was presented last year, you recall it?"

"Sure." It had been quite a big do at the town hall. The Cutler Quilt Guild ladies created a small hanging quilted banner commemorating the 100 years the plant had been making candy and presented it to the Baxters.

"Right. Well near as I can figure, someone ripped it down, balled it up, stepped outside the office, and threw it down onto the factory floor." He rubbed his bald head, causing it to turn slightly pink. "Now that's foolish, that is, but it doesn't speak to premeditation, if you take my meaning."

44

"I'm with you." Jimmy leaned forward, listening intently.

"That thing fell into the warmer machinery. Now that factory being as old as it is and not automated or anything, you got your cogs turning," he held out his hands and intertwined his fingers, "and the cogs mesh together to turn. This piece runs 24/7, something to do with keeping the chocolate soft, it doesn't take much power or need to be watched normally. That banner thing flew into the wheels and, of course, the cogs are made of steel so they kept right on turning, chewing the bejesus out of that material. But then once it had gone over the top and started being pulled down the other side, the fabric started to slow the machine down, just enough to throw off the cogs. You follow?"

Jimmy nodded.

"Right. So, at that point, sparks started to fly off the metal hitting metal. Most of them were harmless, burned out and went to the floor. But the way I see it, a couple of them hit the wiring and caused a short and melted down to where hot electrical wires hit the gas line down by the floor. That caused the explosion. Honest to God, it was a freak series of events; you could never have planned such a thing."

He shook his head sadly. "I figure old Fred knew every sound that old place made and heard the change. He probably left his booth and started walking toward the sound."

He looked at the Chief. "See, the person who threw that piece of material down could have been long gone, probably took the better part of ten minutes or so for this to happen.

They likely never knew. That's why I'm glad I'm not you, son. You got your criminal mischief that led to arson that led to manslaughter." He reached into the bag and pulled out a sad looking plastic package of shredded fabric.

"There she is. I got pictures and all; you can hold on to it if you think there'll be a case to present in court. I'd just as soon you be responsible for it."

Jimmy stood as the fire marshal stood. "That's good work, Dick. I was thinking we might have to call in an outside fire specialist."

Dick grinned his gap-toothed smile. "You still might want to do just that. The insurance might be a bitch. Might need to call in the state investigators. Won't hurt my feelings either way."

He closed the door behind him.

Jimmy sat back down and eyed the sad soggy mess which bore little resemblance to the pristine white piece that he remembered.

There had been a center square with the CC logo and "100 years" and the border had squares with representations of all the types of candy they made. Carl Baxter had to wipe his eyes as he accepted it with his sons by his side. Then he'd had it hung in his office. Jimmy didn't remember Angela being there but then everyone knew she wasn't the sentimental type.

He wondered if he should have told her not to leave town. Dick was right; it was no fun being him right now. He hoped to God he could find her if push came to shove.

He turned the preliminary reports back over and reviewed the initial feedback from the EMTs. When the alarm sounded, Penny Harten and Mike Sharp jumped into the rescue truck and beat the fire trucks there by about five minutes. Knowing, as everyone else did, that Fred Smith should be there, they spent those minutes searching for him even before they joined the team to make sure the gas was off.

Jimmy scanned quickly to find what he wanted to find. Fred's injuries and the position in which they found him, face up with burns primarily on the front of his body, indicated that he was walking toward the explosion, not running away from it.

Jimmy muttered. "Thank the Lord for small favors." That felt wrong so he added, "Good job, Fred. Rest in peace, my friend."

He sat there for a minute with his eyes closed, beyond tired. When he took this job, he expected to be bored, handing out tickets and putting the occasional drunk into a cell. He was not qualified for bigger crimes. He also knew there was no one else in Cutler who was any more qualified for this job—except Gabe Downing.

It was Gabe who had, when they met for a late breakfast the day following the explosion after they'd each had a few hours of sleep, pointed out the security cameras on several businesses nearby, including the Spring Bar which would still have been open at the time of the explosion. In fact, it had lost a couple of its front windows in the blast. Jimmy unashamedly took notes. Brilliant, he thought.

"Now none of these cameras is going to show you who did it. They're too far away and it was dark. But what you might be able to figure out is whether or not there are any vehicles that were there half an hour before and were not there at the actual time of the explosion. That's a pretty narrow window and nobody in Cutler's out moving a vehicle at that time of night."

Jimmy nodded.

Gabe ran a hand through his white hair and took a breath. "Okay, so the first people you need to interview and alibi out are all three Baxters, of course. You can also interview anyone who might have had a view of the factory, like that block of apartments up on the hill to the south. You never know, you might find an insomniac or night worker who saw a light inside the plant."

Jimmy looked at Gabe and the older man saw the signs of mental and emotional overload. "Tell you what. If you want me to use my auxiliary status, I could take statements from the Baxters."

The Chief managed to keep his face composed but the gratitude shone in his eyes.

Twelve

Gabe left the office and went straight to Dennis Baxter's address, a brick home in one of the older developments on a hill by the high school. His wife greeted Gabe, asked him to call her Jasmine, and offered him coffee which she served in a sturdy mug that said "Cutler's Candies" on the side.

He took it gratefully and sat on the flowered sofa while she went to find Dennis. The living room was filled with family photos and a large portrait of Carl Baxter had pride of place over the sofa. The furnishings told Gabe that, if Dennis had been making a fair amount of money, he hadn't been spending it on a luxury home.

When Jasmine came to show Gabe into Dennis's home office, the man stood to shake hands without coming out from behind his desk. It was a position of safety, Gabe recognized. The room itself was wood paneled with library shelves on three walls and a fireplace on the other. Gabe felt like he had stepped back into the fifties or perhaps into a Sherlock Holmes novel.

Papers were strewn over the desk. Dennis smiled as he caught Gabe looking around. "This was my parents' house." He shrugged. "Dad lived here with us until...I guess we haven't changed it much."

"No need if it feels like home," Gabe murmured. Then he volunteered that he was acting in an official police

49

capacity to take a statement from Dennis. If Dennis preferred, they could go to the station. Otherwise, Gabe would record their conversation, it would be typed up formally, and an email acknowledgement would be accepted.

The tall pale man looked appalled at the idea of going to the station exactly as Gabe had expected. They both knew it would be all over town that he had been "hauled in" for questioning within hours.

Gabe kept his questions simple and to the point, watching for reactions on the bristly face and in the tired eyes. Dennis said that he was at home in bed, like everyone else, when the factory exploded. He said his wife could verify that if necessary. When the "boom" came, they both sat up and he jumped out of bed immediately.

"How do you feel about the explosion?"

Dennis shook his head, swallowed, and his eyes filled. "To be honest, Gabe, I don't give a damn about the plant. I understand that my Dad spent his whole life there and his father before him and it's rough that this has happened so soon after Dad left us.

"But what I'm having trouble with is Fred being…killed. I wish I could fix that more than anything. He should have retired, obviously, but he and Dad went back decades and my sense was that he needed the money. Given a little time, I would have arranged a pension for him so he could have just done his volunteer work with the Vets." He looked at Gabe and closed his eyes to keep the tears at bay. Then he sighed. "I swear. That's what I would have done."

His voice choked and Gabe knew that Dennis was having a hard time talking about it. But he had a couple more questions.

"I have to ask, do you have any idea who might have done this?"

After the slightest hesitation, Dennis shook his head.

Gabe stood up. "One more thing then. How do you honestly feel about the plant and its future? Do you want it to stay open?'

Dennis almost smiled. "In this town, that could be construed as a trick question, Gabe. It has always been my intention to keep it going, not just for my family's sake, not for Dad, but for Cutler. Between you and me, I'm sick of the smell of chocolate." He swallowed. "I intend to change things up into something more environmentally sound, more green. But I will never let the plant close; I can't put these people out of work. I hope that answers your question."

Gabe thanked Dennis for his time, and left for Clark's.

Clark was single and lived in one of the new developments outside of town. Each home was carefully modeled to look like a classic city brownstone.

He answered the door and ushered Gabe inside. It felt dark and stately, the man himself turned out immaculately.

"What can I do for you?" He asked immediately, not offering Gabe a seat. After Gabe asked if he could sit, Clark perched on the edge of one of two reading chairs in front of the fireplace. He didn't appear to be the least bit rattled by recent events.

He only became disgruntled at the idea of being taken down to the station and readily agreed to give a statement to Gabe.

"Where were you when the plant exploded?"

It seemed such a simple and obvious question that Gabe was surprised when Clark hesitated to answer. He sat up straighter and paid attention.

"I was with a friend." Clark was now looking at the floor, clearly not wanting to meet Gabe's eyes.

"We'll need a name and address or phone number so we can verify that," Gabe said quietly.

"Is that really necessary?" Clark's hands gripped the knees of his pants tightly, wrinkling the smooth fabric.

"Is it a problem?"

"Do you know what this town is like, Mr. Downing?"

Gabe smiled. "I'm getting there."

"So, if I give you a name, the whole town will know before the end of the day."

Gabe threw the man a warm look. "What makes you think they don't already?"

To his credit, Clark laughed.

When Gabe asked him next if he had any idea who might have done this to the plant, Clark did not hesitate.

"None."

"One last question. How do you feel about the plant? Do you want it to stay open?"

Clark hesitated. "I always wanted to be an architect, if I'm being honest. I started classes but then Dad got upset." He took a breath. "Having said that, I will support Dennis in keeping the plant open for the town. I won't abandon him or Cutler." He shrugged. "We can't all run away." He grinned.

Having completed that interview, Gabe phoned Angela at the number he had been given. He asked her if they could Facetime or Zoom so that he could record the interview.

"No. I don't like to use those things. I'm in New York, I'm staying here, and I've done nothing wrong."

"So I will have to notify Chief Haynes that you refuse to account for your whereabouts the night of the explosion," He said firmly.

"I didn't say that. I was here; you can check with my doorman. But I'm sure as hell not coming back to Cutler and facing that town. Do you have any idea what it's like?"

"Yes, I think I do."

"Well, that's it then." She gave him the number for the front desk of her building and told him to ask for Ralph, then she hung up.

Gabe hadn't even had a chance to ask her the question he had asked her brothers about the future of Country Candies but he didn't really have to; her answer seemed fairly obvious.

Gabe dropped the tapes off to the station. As with so many interviews he had conducted throughout his career, he had found out some information that was needed and some information he wished he could forget.

But at least they had paper in the files for the investigators. Not that any of it clarified who had actually caused the explosion.

Dennis's alibi was his wife. Clark's alibi was a "friend" who preferred to remain anonymous although Gabe was fairly confident he could find out who it was in about five minutes if he tried. Angela's was the most solid and she could, perhaps, have slipped the doorman a hundred bucks to lie for her. It was paper but it was a whole lot of nothing.

If he'd had to charge one of them right away, it would have been the sister. She seemed a rather nasty piece of work and he could think of several motives---frustration, anger, revenge, money.

The only problem was that a court demanded evidence.

The person responsible for the explosion at the candy factory had never intended to kill anyone. Their hands shook as they read the Cutler paper and realized what they had done. Their next thought was what could they do to make it go away?

Thirteen

Those first couple of days, Jimmy and his part-time deputy put in long hours but he felt that they had done a good job. While Joe did the leg work of conducting interviews in the area, Jimmy obtained and went through security footage from six different cameras. As he was about to give up, he noticed something on the surveillance tapes from the Spring Bar across the street from the factory that caused him to lean forward in his chair.

There was a shiny black truck parked up the street from the factory. Off hand, he couldn't think of anyone in town who owned such a nice and new truck. He tried to zero in on the plates but all he could make out was color. It sure wasn't the PA plate with its white center and blue and yellow border strips; it was a solid tan with black numbers. New Jersey? According to the time stamps, it was there an hour before and gone by the time the plant blew up.

His heart had raced for a bit.

Then Trixie caught a look at the picture as he printed it out.

"Hey, I know that truck!" She grinned.

Now it had been confirmed that the truck belonged to Chuck Martin's brother who came to visit from Jersey. When Chuck found out he'd parked his truck on the street, he made him move it. He'd shown it to Trixie and her husband when they came over for dinner.

Potential witness interviews, 22 in all, revealed nothing.

Jimmy knew it was time to move on to the next round which was going to be much harder than the first. Who stood to gain? He would have to figure that out. Was it the development firm that wanted the land? Rumors had been flying for months that the land was of interest for condos that would definitely sell quickly because of Cutler's proximity to the big university up the interstate. There were other rumors that the university itself wanted the land.

There were three realtors in town. He'd need to speak to each of them. The fact that he knew them all well made it harder so he started with the easiest first.

Mark Murphy, whose wife Diane taught at the high school and was Miranda Downing's best friend, came down to the station as soon as Jimmy called.

They talked about the Eagles, the Steelers and the Pirates before the chief could bring himself to ask the big question.

"Are you aware of any company trying to buy the factory so they could tear it down and redevelop it?"

Mark sighed. "I wish I weren't. Like everyone else in town, I don't like the idea of losing the jobs at the factory. But I've heard about one from Philly, in particular, the Lyman Group, but they didn't come to me. I just found out through the grapevine."

"Anything else I should know?"

The man across the desk swallowed hard.

"Come on, Mark. This is arson and manslaughter."

Mark nodded. "I know. Poor old Fred. Well, please don't say you heard it from me but I have some sense that Marlo Perkins isn't doing so well. People say she cuts corners and, you know, takes advantage of people from out of town, and stuff like that. She'll do about anything to get a sale and word gets around when you work like that. I certainly don't like seeing her name on a contract anymore." He looked ashamed to speak ill of another realtor. "I heard she was making inquiries to the Baxters on behalf of the Lyman Group."

He gave an "in for a penny, in for a pound" shrug. "I looked them up. They're not good people. I would hate to see them come to Cutler."

"I appreciate your honesty."

They shook hands and Mark left.

Marlo Perkins. She and Jimmy had dated briefly in high school until he found out that their relationship was far from exclusive. She had long since married and divorced and remarried and divorced. The Chief decided to wait until tomorrow to contact Marlo.

57

Fourteen

I straightened the collar of my black suit. It was hard to believe it was only two weeks since I'd worn it last. Gabe stepped behind me and laid his warm hands on my shoulders, meeting my eyes in the mirror. I turned into his arms for a hug.

I felt like I was seeing the same faces in the Roman Catholic Church as had been at the Baxter funeral, give or take a few. To my surprise, I spotted a contingent from Canterbury Commons, the assisted living community, including Nell Elliot, her short white head wedged between two taller women. It took me a few minutes to identify them as members of the Council that was now running the Commons. I stifled an inappropriate grin.

Nell was small and delicate-looking in a way that belied the fact that she was as sharp as a tack and a professional pick pocket before taking up residence at the Commons. I had come to know her when corruption in the administration came to light last year. She had a good heart really but also was easily bored and had fast fingers.

Surely they didn't think that Nell would pick pockets at a funeral but I couldn't blame them for trying to make sure.

As if she could sense the look, Nell turned her head and flashed me a grin, then shook her head slightly.

The family entered last and slid into the first two rows. Melody Hutchins and her daughter Heather; Fred's younger brother Michael, leaning on a cane, Michael's son John and his family of five. A few extras, probably cousins, made it a respectable family showing.

Over the years, I have attended services at all four churches in Cutler and I knelt, stood, and sat through the Mass with familiarity. I felt, rather than saw, Gabe hesitate a second behind, and the thought occurred to me that we had never really discussed religion. He had fallen in with my plans to marry in the Episcopal Church; it had never been an issue. I made a mental note to ask him later about his religious upbringing and preference. Would I ever know everything about the man I married?

Fred's mass was the old one in Latin and it felt appropriate to his age, somehow. Father O'Shea's sermon was warm and heartfelt. It always struck me hard when it was apparent that the presiding minister didn't even know the person being interred.

But it was clear that this silver-haired and dignified priest, I could have sworn I saw tears in his eyes, knew Fred and knew him well. He spoke of his service, his family, his work ethic, and his work with veterans in the community. His eulogy echoed my own feelings that this kind old man should have died in his bed, although he didn't say it in those words. Everyone nodded their agreement and there were sniffles and tissues.

When the closing Ave Maria floated down from the organ and choir loft above us, the casket, accompanied by six Vets in uniform, moved slowly down the aisle.

Father O'Shea followed it, pausing to speak to family and those friends on the aisles as he passed.

Given the chilly wind that raced over the open space, many of the older folks skipped the brief graveside ceremony and moved on directly to the church hall.

Gabe and I went home and had a quick cup of coffee and split a sandwich so we wouldn't show up at the hall ravenous. It seemed gauche, somehow, as if one went to the service to get to the food spread. It reminded me of how folks started to twitch if an actual wedding ceremony went on too long and hurried to the reception for eat and drink. If the buffet or bar wasn't open quickly enough, the grumbling started.

So, by the time we got there, the place was packed. I made my way to Melody and took her hand.

"If there's anything…"

Melody smiled sadly. "Thanks, Miranda. I know you mean that. I may call you…after." She squeezed my hand. "Please help yourselves, if you can." Glancing at the buffet line, she shook her head.

"We're fine, really. I think we'll just say hello to a few folks and head home."

"I envy you." The woman whispered. "I'll be here until the food and drink are gone, I guess."

"It's hard, I know, but you've done a lovely job for Fred. It feels like this is exactly what he would have wanted." I pointed to the Veterans in uniform and the factory workers who had turned out for Fred.

"Oh, I hope so." Melody had tears in her eyes. "I knew his time would probably come soon but this was just so…sudden."

"I understand. You're never really prepared."

"Thanks."

I gave her a final warm look and moved away. I found Gabe surrounded by the Ryans, the family he worked with at their shop in town and whom he seemed to have adopted and vice versa. The family spoke in quiet voices with Gabe about the old man they had known most of their lives. Along with Mr. and Mrs. Ryan, four of their sons were there; their oldest, Max, was working out of town.

I joined them for a few minutes, then touched Gabe's arm. As he tried to steer us through to the door, I felt a hand on my elbow and turned to face Nell.

"Miranda!" The little woman gave me a warm hug.

I resisted the urge to check my pockets (and my watch and earrings).

Nell laughed. "You're all right, sweetie. No work at the funeral."

I breathed a sigh of relief. "Good. How are you?"

"I'm good."

"Did you know Fred?"

Nell nodded. "He came out to us from time to time, visiting some and bringing a treat now and then. He was partial to the Veterans."

I was puzzled. "Are you a Vet, Nell?"

She got a grin at that. "Surprises you, huh? Two tours in Vietnam, for all my sins, as the English say."

"I bet your life story would make a great TV movie."

"Well, a lot of it's classified." Nell winked, then her wrinkled little face went sober. "Can I ask a favor?"

I hesitated, then nodded. I could always say no if she was asking for an alibi or something.

"When I go, will you make sure I have a sendoff like this?"

"Oh Nell. For heaven's sake…"

A small hand was raised and Nell shook her head. "No need for that. I know I'm not going to live forever, my dear. But there are so few people I can trust." She swallowed. "It's not the money, I've got that."

I felt the emotions of the day rising to my eyes. "Having a sendoff like this only requires that you do all the good you can while you're here, Nell. I know you have some…issues…but I also saw how you tried to protect the folks out at Canterbury. That won't be forgotten."

The bright blue eyes sparkled. "Do you really think anyone will come?"

"I guarantee it."

"Thanks." Nell quickly turned into the crowd.

I understood. My feisty little friend wasn't one for emotional scenes. On the way to the car, I told Gabe about Nell's request.

"You'll be my backup to help me make sure it happens for her, okay?"

He smiled down at me. "I will always be your backup."

Once we were safely ensconced in the blessedly quiet car, he added, "So I'm thinking we'll drive over to Bernton and eat somewhere new?"

Getting out of town had definite appeal.

Fifteen

My phone rang as we drove.

"Hey, Queenie. Some turn out, huh?"

"Sure was, and well deserved. But I have some other news."

Something in her voice sobered me even more. "Okay."

"It's about that centenary quilt banner we made for Carl last year."

"Sure, I remember. Candy blocks and such."

"Right." I heard her clear her throat. "Turns out it was the quilt that caused the explosion."

Stunned into momentary silence, I could only gasp. I then put the phone on speaker. "I'm putting you on speaker for Gabe."

"That's fine. I'm just so upset and I know it has nothing to do with the guild, not really."

"Of course you are. How on earth..."

Queenie sighed. "Someone tore the quilt down from the office and threw it over the railing. According to Sally Dixon, Dick's wife, it got caught in the machinery, one thing led to another and sparks hit a gas line."

"Oh my."

Gabe shook his head while I tried to form words. "But that means that whoever did it..."

"May have had no idea what they'd done."

"Holy Lord. What a nightmare. Someone out there not only blew up the factory but…hurt Fred without knowing?"

"Right. I'm just so upset. It's wrong, just wrong, and awful."

"I know, sweetie. It's going to take a while to digest this."

"You got that right."

"Gabe and I are on our way to Bernville right now. But would you like to come over later for a light supper?"

"I'd like that, thanks, Miranda."

"Sure. It's 1 now, how about around 6?"

"Great."

We finished the ride in silence and I found my appetite had diminished a bit. So we settled for a lighter lunch at a diner called Annie's where we both actually ordered salads.

When we got back, I went for a nap while Gabe went into his office to check his emails and see if any client work had popped up. In addition to his fairly new avocation to working in wood, he does private security and investigation work now and then, mostly for existing and well-known clients who have become close friends over the years. His FBI background got him the work initially but now he enjoys the occasional chance to keep his skills intact.

I woke refreshed, showered, and came out of the bedroom to find my husband prepping our meal. He had made a quick run to the market and was making steak and baked potatoes, not the light supper I had in mind but, he reminded me, one of Queenie's favorite comfort meals.

I pitched in by setting the table and, before I knew it, there was a light knock and Queenie came in through the back door (as everyone else does).

I quickly gave my taller red-haired friend a hug and we sat down directly at the table while Gabe finished off the steaks. The sight of the pile of potatoes, sour cream and butter brought a wan smile to Queenie's face.

We talked about Fred's service and waited for Queenie to bring up the quilt. When she did, I asked, "Do you have it? Have you seen it?"

Queenie shook her head. "All I know is that Dick brought it to Jimmy a couple of days ago. It's probably under wraps as potential evidence." Her eyes filled. "I know I'm overreacting but losing Carl and then Fred, the factory, the jobs, even the quilt we made that Carl was so proud of..."

"I understand. It's overwhelming." Then I added, "You know, honey, it seems likely that the person didn't deliberately use the quilt. It might have just been handy."

I don't think that helped much. No matter what I said, tossing our handiwork around like an old oil rag was disrespectful and just mean. I didn't know how to work around that. Thankfully, my husband was better at it.

Gabe, sitting next to Queenie, put his arm around her and gave her a squeeze. Then, unexpectedly, he said, "How about dessert?"

Both of us looked at him and then started to laugh. The guy really knows how to break a mood and how to get our attention.

66

"Strawberry shortcake!" He announced and small sighs escaped from both of us.

He hopped up and served the dessert and fresh coffee.

As Queenie got up to leave, I took her arm and looked her in the eye. "If we get the chance, we'll fix it." I added firmly, "and if it's beyond fixing, we'll make another one."

Queenie nodded and managed a smile. It seemed that the assurance, the dose of normality, and perhaps sugar, was what Queenie needed and she looked much better when she left to go home.

I spent an hour in my sewing room working on a set of three baby quilts for Zoey's babies, restoring my faith in quilting as therapy and dispelling the sad idea of our quilt doing harm.

Sixteen

After much discussion, Dee and I decided to return to Sylvia's for lunch the next day. We had to get back to normal and avoiding her didn't feel right. There were a few light snow flakes falling and wetting my face as I walked over.

When Dee rolled into the booth, I recognized at once the "I know something" look on her face. It hadn't changed much since we were six.

Sylvia set down two coffees that I had ordered. "Today we have the meatloaf and mashed potatoes and a chef salad with homemade bread on the side."

We stared up at her, waiting for the comment Sylvia usually made about how some could use a salad now and then. Or any other smart remark aimed at Dee. Silence.

Sylvia managed a small smile. "Okay, two meatloafs."

Dee sighed. "Do you think I should say something smart just to get her jumpstarted?"

I shook my head. "Doesn't sound like a good idea right now. So what's going on?"

Dee lowered her voice. "Mark got a call from Jimmy. He actually went to the station and Jim asked him about any developers who might have approached Mark about the factory."

"Ohmigod. Mark wouldn't be involved in anything like that." I chuckled. "Lord, I'm trying to imagine Mark sneaking around the candy factory so he can get a contract to sell it to an outside company. I mean, really?"

Dee grinned. "Yeah, right?" She shook her head. "If he was gonna go for the big score, I wish he'd done it before we had two boys in college, you know."

"I hear you. So is he interviewing other realtors too?"

"Uh huh. At least he's going to. There's only Cynthia Corten, you know, and frankly, she's a bit long in the tooth to be plotting. And Marlo Perkins." Dee wrinkled her nose. "I don't know why he didn't just go straight to her. You know about that family."

"Yes, and I've always thought it was a bit unfair to judge all of them by their dad's actions."

Dee snorted. "Yeah, right. The sins of the fathers and all that. But I've actually met the woman and believe me, it's not just that she's a Perkins. There's something off there." She narrowed her eyes and waved her hand in a corkscrew gesture.

"Interesting, no?" I answered with a grin. "What happened was plain awful and I know that. I think we can also believe that poor Fred was in the wrong place and all. But I just wish we could move forward with some decisions. There are so many lives at stake here."

Sylvia placed the dishes in front of us and I shut my mouth immediately. I looked up to see tears in her eyes. "Amen, sister."

I reached out and squeezed the worn hand and Sylvia quickly retreated into the kitchen.

I took a breath and looked at my best friend. "Hey, Queenie's going to schedule a quilt lesson for free at the shop one night. Want to come?"

Dee's mouth fell open as if I'd said aliens were landing. "Uh, not really."

I rather enjoyed that. "Think about it. You're always complaining that you miss out on stuff because you're not in the guild." Oh yes, she did. Or she invited herself on every trip the guild took.

"You have a point there. Maybe I will." Dee grinned and, as I had intended, the tension was broken. But I wasn't going to hold my breath waiting for her to show up to that lesson.

Seventeen

The insurance investigators were on their way.

Jimmy wished he had completed his interviews with the realtors. But Cynthia had gone out of town for the weekend and Marlo hadn't been at Fred Smith's funeral or he might have approached her there to ask her to come into the station. Or he might be avoiding her as long as possible.

When they showed up Monday afternoon, they stuck out like a couple of sore thumbs or like strangers in suits, and, before dark, most everyone knew there were two of them, a man and a woman, and they had checked into the Hilton off the Interstate out by the mall.

They got to the factory as light was fading around 4. They took some pictures at a safe distance from the muck and it was clear they didn't intend to get their hands dirty. That made it feel like there was a foregone conclusion on one of their laptops to anyone who happened to pass by.

The next morning they made their way to the police station. Jimmy showed them into the interrogation room; his office didn't have room for two extra people.

They politely shook hands, introduced themselves, sat down, and waited. Jimmy opened the folder which contained copies of the reports.

"First, we have the preliminary findings of our fire marshal. It has been hard to pinpoint the exact starting point of the fire. It seems to be a rather complicated matter. There certainly was an explosion." He added, clearing his throat, "no ignition switch, signs of fire starter, or clear sign of arson has been found."

They glanced at the report, then back at him.

"Second, as you may be aware, the owner of the plant passed away several weeks ago and left it to his three children as equal shareholders. Interviews were conducted with each of them and their locations at the time of the explosion have been verified. Copies are provided."

He looked for any reaction. The woman nodded and managed a tight smile which he chose to take as encouragement.

"Third, interviews were conducted with 22 individuals who might have had line of sight of the factory that evening. Since they produced no viable evidence, a summary is included. The individual interviews are available if needed."

This time, he moved right along.

"Fourth, all security cameras within the area were reviewed and the footage screened for any signs of an intruder. No such footage was found. A listing of the cameras and their locations is included."

The man, who introduced himself as Howard Richmond, spoke. "This seems to have been a pretty good start to the investigation, Chief Haynes." He softened his tone. "Are we correct in understanding that a man was killed in this...incident?"

Jimmy sighed. "The security guard, Fred Smith, who was stationed in a small booth just outside the plant, sustained injuries consistent with the scenario that he heard something out of the ordinary inside the plant and was walking toward the machinery when it exploded."

The female investigator, Ellery Reddick, pulled a water bottle from her tote and took a drink.

Wrapping up, Jimmy told them that he had asked for a team of special investigators from the state police to come in and take a look. They were expected in another day or two.

The only time they perked up was when Jimmy advised that he was currently investigating whether an outside firm might have had an interest in obtaining the property for new development. They exchanged glances but quickly returned to their stoic behavior.

They all stood. "Please extend our condolences to the family," Ms. Reddick said quietly.

Then they gave him business cards and asked to have the final reports forwarded. The whole meeting took less than 30 minutes. Then the investigators stopped for a quick lunch at Sylvia's, speaking only to place their order, and went over to Mayfield Insurance, where their meeting lasted a bit longer.

Suddenly, Adam Mayfield had replaced the Baxter's attorney as the most popular guy in town. He confided to his wife that the Cutler Candy insurance policy, which had been updated only three times in the past fifty years, did not cover arson. Any insurance that might have provided a benefit for Fred's death was also null and void if it was proved to have occurred as a result of arson. To her credit, Carrie knew better than to ask for details and not to discuss the case with anyone.

But after Adam left the office, the two women who worked in his office wasted no time peeking into the file on his desk. By the time the insurance adjusters were on their way back to Philly, everyone in town but Dennis Baxter was pretty sure there would be no insurance money coming to rebuild the factory.

Dennis got a form letter by email the following day that said, pending the final reports from the state police investigators and a final determination of deliberate arson possibly at the behest of a third party, no claim would be paid on the Cutler Candy factory.

Dennis met with his brother and called his sister to let her know.

Clark wasn't surprised. "We're going to have to decide what to do." He said sadly. "Do you really want to rebuild?"

He and Dennis discussed options, then they both stayed on the line to call their sister.

Angela said, "Fine. So it's done. Dad said we couldn't sell the plant. Well, it's pretty much destroyed now. So we can tear down what's left and sell the land, right?"

The conversation took a turn and ended in an impasse.

As soon as she put her phone down it rang again. Clark. "Hello."

"All right Ang, now what?"

"I'm sure I don't know what you mean."

"Cut the crap! I know you did this."

Angie thought hard for about five seconds. "Huh. That's funny because I thought that you did it."

She heard her brother catch his breath. "What? Are you serious? Look, I want to do something else with my life but not enough to blow up our legacy and kill Fred! It's you, all you want is the money." He said accusingly. "Are you saying you didn't pay Fred and didn't sabotage the machinery?"

"Yes, brother dear, I am saying exactly that and it saddens me that you could even think that. Goodbye, Clark, and don't ever call me again."

She put down her phone and a slow smile spread across her lips, then it faded.

Something was going to have to be done. And she knew just the person to do it.

David Fleisher wasn't a good man and she didn't care for him much. But she made the call anyway.

"Mr. Fleisher, I thought you should know that your daughter's still seeing Clark Baxter behind your back. They're just waiting for you to move to Florida so they can live together, maybe even get married." She paused to let the man hyperventilate and explode. Then she finished, "So what are you going to do about it?"

Eighteen

Cynthia Corten had just gotten back into town.

"Hey Jimmy. Cynthia. I heard you were speaking to local realtors. Shall I come over?"

He grinned. It was unusual for someone to ring up and volunteer to come in for an interview. But CC, as she liked to be called, was no shrinking violet.

She was somewhere between 65 and 80 and anyone in town who knew for sure knew enough to keep quiet about it. Her record in real estate was spotless, her dealings completely above board.

Maybe he was avoiding Marlo but he told himself he was just covering the bases. After all, in the mysteries he (and Lucy) loved to read, wasn't it always the very least likely suspect? Of course, the fact that Cynthia had a cast on her foot and was using a cane dampened that theory. Dare he hope she was faking? That thought brought a smile to his face as the 95-pound woman took a seat across from his desk.

"Jimmy, darling, how are you? Ready to buy a house for Lucy Huntley yet? She's always loved the old Planter place outside of town you know. Sure, it's a fixer upper now but that means I can get you a great price." Her keen blue eyes peered at him.

"Thank you, Cynthia, but that's not what we're here to talk about."

She sighed. "I know. Poor Fred. We went to school together, you know." Catching herself, she quickly added, "Of course, he was years ahead of me."

"Of course. Now I have to ask you if you've had any contact with outside developers interested in buying the factory so they can tear it down and redevelop it."

She waved a wrinkled red-tipped hand. "Oh, honey, about every other year, it comes up. I've reached out to Carl half a dozen times but he is," she caught herself, "was, a stubborn old cuss."

Jimmy's eyes widened. It wasn't the response he had expected.

"In fact, my dear, you don't need to look too far. There's a few folks up at the university who wanted to take that land and use it for some kind of research facility to do with the water. Environmental or agriculture or such." She pulled a couple of sheets of paper from her large handbag. "Here, I wrote down a few names and numbers for you. But I wouldn't get my hopes up, honey." She pointed a bony finger at the paper. "My understanding is that those folks are talking to Connors Creek further upstream on the other side of the campus. That town's all but dead and they'll be real happy to get those jobs, you see." She grinned and her perfect teeth were very white. "I wouldn't expect you to catch those folks blowing up the candy factory."

"I appreciate the info. Thanks for coming in."

"Always good to see you." She struggled to her feet and then leaned over the desk. He could see a lot more wrinkles as she got closer and he sort of automatically drew back, then made himself lean closer to hear her.

"One hates to speak ill of a colleague and all that but I hope you're going to talk to Marlo Perkins." She shook her head. "No good, any of those Perkins. Her old man ripped off some folks and bought up their land cheap for his farm without a thought. But I can tell you from personal experience, she's pulled some pretty underhanded stunts and should have lost her license by now. If anyone would be involved with dirty tricks, she's your girl." She sighed heavily. "Not that I don't feel bad for her. There's just not that much real estate traffic in this town and you know how it is when people hear your name and turn the other way. Not many have been willing to give her the benefit of the doubt, if you see what I mean." She shrugged. "It's a small town with a long memory."

Jimmy nodded. "For sure."

After she left, he made the call to Marlo, accepting the fact that he couldn't put it off any longer. Then he made a second call.

Nineteen

Taylor Perryman had seen enough. For the last several days, she'd been building up a head of steam and somebody was going to get an earful. Pushing her two-year old daughter in her stroller, she marched into the Mayor's office.

The woman behind the desk outside the Mayor's office greeted her familiarly. She came out and bent down to lay a hand on Noelle's soft curls and got a wet toothy grin back.

But Taylor was determined not to soften her attitude. "I need to see Sandy," she said fiercely.

Christine stood up and nodded, taking in the expression on Taylor's face. She quietly opened the door and went in.

"Chris, I told you I'm busy. What is it?" Sandy brushed a piece of hair out of her eyes and looked up from her computer.

"I know. I'm sorry. But Taylor Perryman's outside and I think it's important."

"Taylor?" The mayor saved her work on the screen and stood up. "Okay, bring her in." She had far too much respect for the widow of the former police chief of Cutler not to see her right away.

"Thanks for seeing me."

The Mayor was also quick to see the distress and determination in the woman's face. "What can I do for you?"

Taylor swallowed. "This has got to stop. The police department has to change." She softened her voice as best she could, glancing at Noelle who sat in the stroller next to her chewing on the edges of her plastic book.

Sandy tried to clear her head of all the other things on her plate and listen. "What are you thinking?"

Taylor pulled out her phone. "I've been doing a bit of research. Other towns our size have five police officers, at least three of which are full time. We need more man-hours, we need training and equipment updates."

Sandy scratched her nose as she often did when she was thinking. "You know, we're kind of dealing with the factory issue right now."

Trying not to choke up, reminding herself to be business like, Taylor nodded. "Of course. That is part of my point. Have you seen Jimmy Haynes?" She swallowed. "I don't want to see him go the way my Jake did." Despite her best efforts, her eyes welled up. "He needs help, training, a day off, for God's sake."

The wheels started turning in Sandy's head. Of course that's where this was coming from. Taylor's husband had died from a heart attack while investigating the town's first murder in years. But she had a valid point. Cutler was changing, had changed, and it had to keep changing to survive. The police department with its three men and one vehicle hadn't changed in decades.

She sighed. "We're going to need to come up with money. New business is coming in, but slowly, and if we lose the candy factory…"

"I understand that. So I am going to go to the quilt guild and ask them to help me form a public support group. If we undertake to solicit funds and activate community support, will you look into any state or federal help we might be able to get?"

Sandy smiled. "I can do that. And I will be at any meeting where you think I can help."

Taylor smiled for the first time. "Thank you. I'm going down to talk to Jimmy right now."

Sandy nodded. "Seems fair that you should let him know help is on the way." Her face fell slightly. "Taylor, just try to remember that these things take time. Try not to get his hopes up for too much too fast. Is Gus back yet?"

Taylor shook her head. "Not yet. You see, that's the problem. With Gus away, there's only Jimmy and Joey; they're short a deputy. Anyone but Jimmy would have called him and told him to cut his trip short. But he wouldn't do that."

"Okay." Sandy stood and stuck out her hand. "Thanks, Taylor. A town like this doesn't work without people getting involved." Her face saddened. "I only wish..."

"Yes, me too."

She took hold of the handle of Noelle's stroller and went out the door.

Twenty

She couldn't seem to let it go. She hadn't liked Dennis's tone or Clark's accusation. So Angela decided to cover her bases a bit more. Offense being the best defense, she made the call.

"Chief Haynes."

"This is Angela Baxter." A woman's voice said in between sobs.

"Angela, are you all right?"

"NO." She cried. "I didn't do this, Jim, I swear."

He sighed. "Calm down. Tell me what you need to tell me. Take a breath."

He heard her do that and then she continued a bit more calmly. "Okay, Dennis said I'd have to come forward. I went to the factory. I was pissed off, I admit it. Dad's will saying that we couldn't sell it, well, he knew how badly I wanted to do just that.

"So I made up my mind to leave. I have a place in the city, you know. I went to the factory one last time to pick up some of my personal things—I had a pair of shoes and some make up and stuff, before I left. I needed to go, no one was actually interested in making this company work, you know?"

"Okay, I understand."

"When I saw that stupid 100 year white thing hanging up in the office, I ripped it down, okay? I admit it. I ripped it down and threw it on the floor. Maybe I stepped on it once or twice." She took a breath, then the tears came back into her voice. "But I didn't throw it into the factory; I'm not an idiot. And I didn't kill Fred, ohmigod, I never…"

"Angela, I'm going to need you to revise your earlier statement covering this. Can you come into the station?"

"NO. I'm in New York and I'm staying here." She paused. "I can't face those people, Jim. I know they'll think I did it. How can I face anyone in Cutler?" She was crying now in earnest and Jimmy actually felt sorry for her.

He certainly couldn't tell her she was wrong. "So can you type up a simple statement as to what you did and email it to me? If this becomes a court case, you'll have to testify in person, there's nothing I can do about that. But, for now, having the information to move the investigation along will be a help."

She hiccupped. "Do I have to?"

"Yes. I'm afraid so."

"Okay. Jim, you believe me, don't you?" She whimpered.

He knew it didn't actually matter if he did or not but he told her he did, anyway, if only to ensure that she sent the statement. He gave her his personal email to send it to so that the whole station would have less chance of seeing it. But this was Cutler and they both knew it would be common knowledge within hours of arrival.

He gave her a warning that she must not disappear but needed to keep him apprised of her whereabouts. She agreed to include her new contact information in the email.

"You will find out what happened, won't you?" She pleaded. "Or, even if I want to, I'll never be able to show my face in town again."

"I'll do my best."

Angela clicked off, took a substantial gulp of her wine, and went into the bedroom to re-do her makeup. Now, at least, if or when her fingerprints were found on that rag, she had it covered.

Her phone rang immediately. When she saw the number, she almost didn't pick up. Honest to God.

"I told you not to call me," she said angrily.

"But I have to go to the police station," Marlo said in a scared voice. "You promised me it wouldn't come to this."

Angela was losing patience fast. Involving this idiot was probably a mistake. Suddenly, she had an idea.

"Listen, honey. I know you're scared. But we're still all right." Angela proceeded to tell Marlo she had everything under control and was taking care of it. "That local yokel has absolutely nothing on you. If you keep it together, you walk away from this. We both do."

It took some more soothing but, when she hung up, Angela actually thought Marlo might pull it off.

Twenty One

Marlo showed up at 1:30 on Wednesday, nervously clutching a tote bag with her picture and the name and address of her real estate office on it. She at least had the sense not to call it Perkins RE but had gone with Hometown Realty.

Gabe Downing had agreed to sit in after Jimmy had given him a quick summary of his conversations with the other two realtors. Marlo's questioning seemed their most promising lead so far. Of course, he also picked up on Jimmy's discomfort and sensed that he didn't want to interview the woman alone.

"Take a seat, Marlo," Jimmy said not unkindly. The woman was wearing too much makeup, her hair was an odd black color, and her cheap suit skirt was about 8 inches too short on her tall frame.

"Thanks." It came out as more of a whisper than she intended and she sat up straight and cleared her throat.

"I need to ask you some questions. Let's start with, have you ever been contacted by an outside developer regarding the candy factory?"

She nodded vigorously. She knew the answer to this one. "Sure. I would expect the other realtors have, too. I had a serious proposal from a firm in Philly. I passed it along to Carl, copied it to Dennis, Clark and Angela, but there didn't seem to be any interest. Now I understand that Carl's will says the children can't sell the place, anyway." She tucked a strand of long black hair behind her ear. "I can't say I'm not disappointed."

Jimmy nodded. "Right. Can you tell me where you were the night of the explosion?"

She looked startled at the bluntness of the question. "Home in bed like everyone else."

Gabe asked quickly, "Alone?"

She colored. "Of course, alone. I live alone." She managed an offended look. "I'm not married."

"So you didn't leave your house at any time that evening?"

"No."

Jimmy turned his laptop screen toward her. "So this isn't you then, walking toward the factory about 11:30?" The security footage from the bar across the street was too blurry to amount to much as evidence. But he was risking it, knowing Marlo probably wouldn't know that.

She paled. Then she leaned forward and peered at the screen. All you could tell was that the figure was tall and thin. She happened to be 5'11" herself and had always been thin. She pointed a chipped nail at the screen. "That could be anyone."

Gabe interjected sternly, "It could be anyone. But is it you?"

She leaned back, away from that voice. "No."

"Do you know the Baxters?"

She shrugged. "It's a small town. The factory is a big deal. And, as I told you, I did try to reach out to them."

"But, socially, do you know Clark?"

"Not really."

"Dennis?"

"No."

She stiffened slightly in her chair in anticipation of the next question.

"Angela?"

She blinked. "I might have met her here or there."

Seeing her reaction, Jimmy followed up, his words heavy with sarcasm, "How? It's not like you run in the same circles."

Her eyes narrowed and her chin rose. "I don't know what you mean by that."

"Well, for one thing, she's gotta be, what 15 years older than you."

"So?"

"And she's a Baxter..." he smirked, "and you're...not."

"Of all the nerve. I'll have you know that I have a lot of friends in what passes for an upper class around here. You don't know what you're talking about."

"Would Angela be one of them? Do you consider her a friend?" He asked quickly.

Marlo was dumbstruck. She stood. "I'm going now."

"How do you feel about the factory being out of operation?"

She smiled snarkily. "I could not care less."

"Did you know that there was a white banner celebrating the plant's 100 years of operation across the back of the factory by the breakroom?"

She snorted. "Shows how much you know. It was in the old man's office."

Jimmy smiled. "Okay, thanks for coming in."

After she was gone, Gabe chuckled. "Nice one on the footage. Where'd you get it?"

The chief smiled. "Oh, it's from the bar across the street from the factory. It just happened to be from two days ago and the guy in the footage is Joey T." He rubbed his hands together. "And she knew where the banner was. How would she know that? I don't remember her saying she had ever been to the factory."

Gabe nodded. "What did you think?"

"I think she's up to her eyeballs in this somehow and she's scared to death."

"I think that's right. Now what?"

"That state investigator mobile lab is on its way tomorrow. If we're really lucky, they'll find her fingerprints on something." He grinned. "We have her prints here. She was charged with shoplifting back in high school."

"Sweet." Gabe smiled. "And there's no reason whatsoever for her prints to be anywhere near that factory."

Jimmy blew out a long breath in relief. "It sure would help move things along…"

As Gabe stood, the door opened and a red-haired man stuck his head in. "Am I interrupting?"

Jimmy jumped up. "Boy, are you a sight for sore eyes, Gus."

The man grinned. "You wait till I leave town to have all the excitement for yourself, I hear."

"I'm willing to share." The chief stuck out his hand. Gus shook it, then turned to Gabe and nodded.

"How are you doing, Gabe?"

"I think we'll all be better now that reinforcements have arrived."

"I came as soon as I heard." The big man chuckled. "Wife's still unpacking the car." John Gustafson had taken a two-week leave to help his daughter move from college to an apartment in Pittsburgh near her new job. "So what can I help with?"

Gabe spoke first. "I'm gonna stick my nose in here and suggest that I bring you up to speed while Jimmy goes home, takes a shower, and makes plans to take Lucy out to dinner." He turned to Jimmy. "See you tomorrow?"

Jimmy knew he should protest but he simply couldn't bring himself to. "I guess it would be good if I checked to see if Lucy's found someone else."

They all laughed.

As Jimmy approached the front door, it swung open and Taylor Perryman came in, the stroller coming after her. He held the door.

"Mrs. Perryman, how can I help you?"

She looked up at the young chief. "I'm here to help you. And call me Taylor."

They went back in and sat down in an empty office. Jimmy wasn't sure what she had to say was for Gabe and Gus to hear.

Her eyes filled as she reminded Jimmy of what had happened to her Jake. He felt a lump in his throat.

89

"That was awful. I'm so sorry."

She swallowed. "Me, too." Her eyes glittered but her jaw was set. "It's not going to happen to you—or any other officer in Cutler." She outlined her ideas and Jimmy was hard pressed to keep the moisture from his own eyes.

"That sounds...amazing." He managed.

"Now Sandy told me not to get you too excited because it might take some time." Her chin rose. "But it's not going to take as long as she thinks. I'm going to enlist the quilt guild."

That brought a smile to Jimmy's unshaven face. "Well that's that done then."

Noelle chose that moment to let them know she agreed and Jimmy planted a kiss on her soft head and spoke a few quiet words back to her while she drooled down her shirt.

As they both stood to go, Jimmy impulsively gave the smaller woman a hug and she returned it.

"It's going to work out," She said firmly, keeping her emotions under control.

Then he and Taylor walked out together. They could hear Gabe filling Gus in on what he had missed. It looked like it was going to take a while.

Twenty Two

Saturday. This being a regular quilt guild meeting, the group usually brought their own work or spent the time researching and sometimes purchasing items for new projects. Queenie had recently initiated a fun "game" for them.

Each quilter brought a bag of scrap strips from 1-3" wide and dumped all the strips into a pile on the cutting table. Each sewer grabbed a handful and a square of white fabric in either a 7 or 8" square size.

Judy Smythin was out of town for a weekend getaway so Brittany and I took two of the machines while Queenie had her usual blue machine. It was just Queenie, Brit, me and Sarah today. Nan, our newest quilter, was showing off her baking skills at a bake-off in Philly today. We were holding the good thought for her.

The group strip pieced a square which only took about 10-15 minutes. Then the squares went back to Sarah who trimmed them even and piled them for joining. In her spare time when the shop was quiet, Queenie would create a pillow, lap quilt, or even a twin quilt and it went into her stockpile to be donated to any worthy cause that approached the shop for an item to raffle off.

The wonderful thing about the strip piece squares was that the patterns were almost limitless! Here is an example:

AUTHOR NOTES FOR QUILTERS:

The four pieces above would make a great pillow. The four squares can form an X or be combined in any number of ways. The size of the strips can be planned so that the centers match up or strips of the same size can be used throughout. This is a great way to incorporate some fun vintage or unique or even those "ugly" patterns in small amounts. Quilters love this style to use up scraps and the end result looks so "intentional."

*You can find instructions for basic string piecing on the internet. One of the best and most fun instructors is Jenny Doan of the Missouri Star Quilt shop. She does a video on string piecing (and any other quilt style you can thing of!)

We piled up the wonderfully random multi-colored squares until break and then settled down to chat and discuss our own projects.

Brittany had brought some baby clothes for me to share with Zoey whom I knew would be thrilled with the handmade pieces. I told them about Michael and Zoey moving. They were all as flabbergasted as I had been. It was a lovely normal guild meeting until Taylor Perryman walked in, pushing Noelle in her stroller.

"May I have a few minutes of your time?"

Surprised but intrigued, there was a universal nod and a chair was pulled up for Taylor. Noelle said a few baby speak words and there were smiles all around. Then she went back to chewing her book and Taylor handed her a teething cookie.

Taylor took a breath. "I've just come from the Mayor's office…"

We listened in sympathetic silence as she talked about how she didn't feel she could stand by and watch Jimmy Haynes work himself to death as police chief. Every woman there knew the horror of Jake Perryman's death on the job. The nods continued.

Queenie spoke for all of us. "How can we help?"

Taylor smiled. "We need community support and we need to raise money. Sandy is willing to try to get some from the state and federal governments. But we have to show that we understand the situation and we will pitch in."

Suddenly I had an idea and it came right out. "I'd be willing to approach Millie Harticutt."

Brittany chirped. "She's definitely the richest person we know." Everyone chuckled as they agreed.

"That would be amazing." Taylor's eyes lit up. "I'll be glad to go with you."

The group started to chatter and before long, the CSLE (Cutler Supports Law Enforcement) committee was formed, first meeting scheduled for Tuesday evening, giving everyone time to absorb the idea and come up with suggestions.

I made good on my own suggestion and called Millie and asked if Taylor and I could stop by to discuss a town matter on Monday. I wanted to be clear that, as much as I enjoyed visiting Millie (and her amazing quilt collection), it was not going to be a strictly social visit. Millie invited us to a light lunch at 1PM.

Gabe and I had a lot to tell each other over dinner that night. Harry seemed in a mellow mood, listening in quietly.

"Taylor Perryman has realized that the police department hasn't changed in a long time and needs to be upgraded." I opened.

Gabe, who had spent time in the worn out facility, agreed immediately. "It's hard to argue with that, isn't it?"

"Absolutely. I don't know how we didn't see it before, you know, after…"

"I know. But it's terrific that she's standing up." He moved me quickly past the sorrow of Jake's passing.

I smiled, knowing exactly what my sensitive husband was doing for me. "It is. Obviously, money is going to be an issue. Sandy is on board to try to get some government funding but we have to all pitch in."

Gabe looked puzzled. "Car washes and garage sales are not going to cut it."

"Nope. So tomorrow Taylor and I are going to have lunch with Millie."

He gave me a hug. "That's my girl. If anyone can help, it will be her."

I suddenly felt a little awkward about asking the woman for money. I realized I had never asked anyone for money before in my entire life. There was a lot riding on this. What if I screwed up?

"I'm not sure I really thought this through. I've never done anything like this before." I said with a frown.

"She's a good person and your friend. She'll understand. She might even be glad you've included her."

That was good. I decided to hold that thought.

Harry put a paw on my knee and I looked down at that sweet little triangle of a furry face.

"Yeooowww." He clearly approved.

"Okay, Harry. I'll do my best."

Twenty Three

We were met at the door by Millie's niece Polly who smiled and led us to the kitchen where the small dining table had been set for four. We shed our hats, coats and gloves onto the hallway coat tree.

She offered us coffee or tea and we gratefully accepted the coffee. As she poured, Millie came in, walking without the cane we had all gotten used to. Her ankle sprain had caused a series of events that led to a change in management at Canterbury Commons. Last year, we discovered that the management had been taking advantage of the residents. I had been heavily involved, along with the rest of the guild and, of course, Diane. We had gotten Millie out of there and some of those running it had been arrested. Millie appreciated our help so she had gifted us each a quilt from her collection. I had been given the most treasured, the award-winning Dollhouse quilt.

"How's the quilt?" Millie smiled.

I felt the blood rush to my cheeks. "It's fantastic. It's still with me; I can't seem to share it yet."

"That's fine, my dear. I know you will always take good care of it."

We really enjoyed the small crust less sandwiches and petit fours which were hardly ever seen in Cutler homes where a peanut butter and jelly sandwich is a regular lunch.

When we exclaimed, Millie waved a hand at Polly. "Turns out my girl here enjoys making such things."

It was Polly's turn to blush but she nodded with a small smile. "I've always wanted to make things like this. I've read about the British high teas and watched them on TV. It's so nice to do something special once in a while."

We were more than surprised by her interest but agreed that it totally made for a special treat.

When we had all put down our napkins, Millie got to the point.

"As pleased as I am to see you, we should probably get down to it. My nap time is coming up."

"Right." Taylor got straight into her explanation that times had changed in Cutler but the police force had not. She had decided to take the lead in trying to get more help, training, and equipment. Currently, there was Jimmy, the chief, full time, and John Gustafson and Joey Traxler, part-time. There needed to be an Assistant Chief so that Jimmy could get a day off, even during an investigation like the one currently going on for the candy factory. They had one police vehicle and their computers were completely outdated. The building itself was a disgrace.

Millie nodded. "News of this project has reached my ears. I understand, of course, Mrs. Perryman, the nature of your own personal interest and you have my deepest sympathy. It is completely understandable that you don't want anyone else to go through what you did.

"I have discussed this matter with Polly. Get the map we were looking at earlier, honey."

To the surprise of her visitors, they found themselves looking at a topographical map of the area.

"I'm moving forward based on the notion that you'd like me to help fund some of these changes." The elderly woman pointed a shaky finger at the map and Polly helped her.

"Polly will be well cared for with the stocks and more liquid assets of the family as well as, of course, this house. But, before you came, I discussed with her an option that would help you and deprive her of little."

Polly nodded. She had come to Cutler with little more than the clothes on her back. In the past few months, she had come to care as much for the community, and her aunt, as for the need for money, which had been her priority all her life. She had struggled for years and now had more security than she had ever known.

Millie sat back down. "Polly has marked on the map and we have here the land deeds showing that I own 50 or so acres, 10 of which reside within the town itself although they are out by the interstate. It's decent enough land but completely undeveloped. We have researched and believe the value, at minimum, to be at least $5,000 an acre. My suggestion would be that the town take into account the need for affordable housing and, as we say, kill two birds with one stone. If the town wants to develop that 10 acres within the town for affordable housing and even a new police station, the remaining 40 acres further out can be sold and the town can have the profits." She added, "But, if affordable housing is to be considered, I want to approve the housing developer that would be chosen so that it would not completely change the character of the town. Understood?"

We nodded, too dazed to even thank her.

She sighed and it was clear that she was tired out. Polly handed the map and papers to Miranda.

"I think she needs to rest now," she whispered. "Call me with whatever you need, okay?"

Completely amazed, Taylor and I could only mumble our heartfelt thanks and I squeezed Polly's hand, trying to express the gratitude we felt. Polly winked and nodded.

Back in the car, we stared at each other and the fortune we held in our hands.

"What do we do now?" Taylor asked, her eyes still wide.

I shook my head to clear the cobwebs. "Well, I know a good realtor."

Back at my desk in the library, I was full of wonder and relief at Millie's generosity. I desperately wanted to call Dee to tell her about the sale that might be coming Mark Murphy's way.

But Taylor and I had decided that Taylor would go over to his office and have him help her figure out the specifics of the land sale. It made sense since I did have a job waiting. The last thing I wanted to do was steal Taylor's thunder although I knew I wouldn't hear the end of it from Dee.

I was sitting there lost in thought when Lucy burst in.

"Jimmy's taking the night off!" The freckles on her pale face glowed and her blue eyes shone. "He's coming over for supper."

"Oh, Lucy. I'm so happy for you. What made him decide to take a break? Is something happening on the case?"

"Gus is back. He's going to hold the fort. Jimmy's already at home, taking a nap and cleaning up. Isn't it wonderful?"

"It is indeed." It occurred to me that it was also a really good idea to make the Chief's job more doable because the young woman who loved him deserved more.

"Hey, it's almost three. Why don't you take off and get ready for your big night?" I raised my eyebrows as I teased the young woman.

"Oh, Miranda." The blush crept up her neck. "Could I really? I do have to shop and..."

"Yes, I'm sure. Now go!"

Lucy blew me a kiss and sprinted out the door.

For another minute or two, I sat there and allowed the memories to sweep over me. When Harry came home from conducting training at the Marine base, I would be that excited, too. Especially after Zoey came, I would be full of things to tell my husband and to show him the amazing things Zoey was doing.

Before I knew it, five o'clock came around so I grabbed my tote bag and went downstairs. I paused at the desk to make sure our volunteers were comfortable locking up at 7. One of them, Jonathan, had been with us awhile now but George was new. I made sure they had my cell number.

"No problem, Mrs. D." Jonathan saluted. "We got this."

I chuckled on my way out. There really was a lot to be said for youthful enthusiasm.

Twenty Four

When Lucy opened the door, a clean and slicked down Jimmy stood there clutching a bouquet. She pulled him inside.

They sat at her small table and ate the dinner she had so carefully prepared: chicken marsala with egg noodles, fresh bread, and apple pie for dessert.

And they talked. It felt like there was so much to say; it had been days since they had exchanged more than a few words. They did not watch TV or listen to music; they sat in the living room and held hands, being together.

Then, without a word, they went into her bedroom and tumbled into bed, holding each other for a while to become reacquainted—first.

Jimmy woke in Lucy's comfortable bed with its quilts and blankets making a cozy nest for the two of them. He allowed himself a moment to just be there, then he turned and kissed her freckled shoulder.

She opened an eye. "What time is it?"

"Just after 7. I have to go."

"Okay," she said sleepily.

"Luce," he said softly, "I want this."

Her smile lit up the morning. "Okay."

He leaned up on one elbow. "I mean it. I want to be with you every morning. I want to marry you."

She giggled and waved her ring finger at him. "I should hope so. You're making payments on this rock."

"I'm serious."

She saw that he was and sat up, her red hair tumbling around her shoulders. "What?"

"As soon as I get through this case, let's set the date."

Her eyes widened. "For real?"

He kissed her then and she knew he meant it.

"There are changes coming to the department. I'm sure you heard about Mrs. Perryman…"

Lucy nodded. "Sure. She's going to raise money so you can get more officers and equipment."

"I'm going to get a full-time Assistant Chief, Luce, so I can work a regular schedule." He smiled down at her. "I'll be around so much you'll be sick of me."

She blinked furiously. "I'll risk it."

Twenty Five

"I cannot believe you didn't call me!"

I heard the outrage in Dee's voice and had been waiting for it, was prepared for it.

"I wanted to, believe me. But it was Taylor's idea to raise money for the police department. She went straight to Mark's office; I had to come back to work." I gave it a beat or two. "But, honey, what a great deal for Mark, huh?"

Dee sighed impatiently. "Of course it is. It will make his, our, year. I guess I understand but I would have expected to hear it from you."

"I know. I'm sorry. I did what I thought was the right thing, not what I wanted to do. I couldn't steal Taylor's thunder like that. This whole thing is her idea."

"Fine. You're buying lunch."

"It's really the least I can do," I answered with a smile in my voice.

"You got that right."

We slid into our usual booth and Sylvia came over. "Today, we have chicken pot pie and barbecue pork sandwiches with homemade chips."

Dee and I looked at each other. "Wow. Tough one."

"I'm sensing barbecue sandwich here," said Sylvia.

With relief, we both nodded.

"You know us so well," I said.

The diner owner smiled. "It's a good thing that you're doing for the police department."

"Thanks," I stuttered.

After she left, I quickly invited Dee to attend the evening meeting of the CSLE group that somehow was already becoming known as "cecil."

My friend's face lit up. She loves to be included and hates missing out on virtually anything. "I can come for an hour. If it lasts longer, I'll have to get over to the school for a parent conference."

We ate, peace restored.

It occurred to me after I was back at work that it was the first time in two weeks we had not discussed the candy factory. Was that a good thing?

Remembering Sylvia's weary face, I wondered.

Later that evening, The CSLE meeting did not go exactly as planned. It seemed every citizen of Cutler considered him or herself invited. So what had been anticipated as a group meeting of maybe 10 or 12 turned into more like 40 or 50.

Taylor spoke first, summarizing the need for the CSLE and how it was intended to help the police department.

Then she called on Polly Stanton to join her at the front of the group. In a quiet voice, Polly announced that her aunt, Millie Harticutt, was donating 50 acres of land, most of which was to be sold for the purpose of funding the police department. She sat back down quickly.

Stunned silence was followed by smiles and cheers. Mark Murphy then took a few minutes to explain the nature of the property and the kind of sale they'd be looking for. He explained carefully that a sale of this size and type might take months to complete. He made sure to confirm that Millie had the final say in determining the buyer of the 10 acres that were to be allocated to affordable homes. But the town also needed to consider carefully who purchased the remaining 40 acres just over the town line.

There were a ton of questions and the Mayor's secretary took notes furiously. Should the police station be torn down? Maybe rebuilt on a piece of the new property?

That one alone blew my mind and I suspect we all felt overwhelmed.

Taylor wrapped up by reminding us that the Harticutt money would only go so far. While she expected to stretch every buck until it broke, she was also expecting the town to show its support as well and would be welcoming ideas on how to show that support. Could one of the car dealers help with a new police vehicle purchase? Could some local contractors chip in to spruce up the station or to build the new one? How about new computer systems-were there any techs in the area who would donate time and training? There were folks with clipboards willing to take names to help with anything and everything.

Finally, Jimmy, Gus and Joey stood and, waving down the applause, Jimmy spoke.

"Thank you all so much. I'm sure you know how much this means to us." He swallowed. "But we have a surprise for Taylor. As part of our new development, we will be instituting the Jake Perryman Scholarship to be awarded each year to any local qualified applicant who wishes to go into the police academy and/or attend law enforcement classes."

He then pulled up a large framed picture of the former chief which he said was going to be hung in the station for all to see.

Taylor burst into tears and was immediately surrounded, then the townspeople moved to the volunteers holding clipboards.

Before the meeting adjourned, Taylor announced that she and the volunteers would review the sign-up sheets and be in touch with those who had signed up. The next meeting was scheduled for one month out.

We had a long way to go but we were now in it together.

Twenty Six

True to her word, Queenie had advertised the free quilt lesson and on Wednesday night, I went over to the shop. Much to her surprise, there were six women there and she knew only three of them.

Queenie explained the basics of quilting: how it started out of a need to use every scrap of fabric, how it became an art form for women whose lives revolved around their homes. She mentioned the fairly recent discovery of exquisite quilts made by a small group of women in an isolated community called Gee's Bend, using and re-using the fabric they had on hand.

She had seen their faces fall at some of the prices in the shop and she wanted them to know that you didn't have to buy yards of expensive new fabric to create a quilt.

She explained to them that the essence of a quilt was the joining of three layers: a top, some form of stuffing or batting, and a backing.

She encouraged them to go home and look at old clothes they might have laying around to see if the fabric could be repurposed. She admitted wryly that she haunted garage sales and thrift shops for clothing to use for the fabric.

She made sure to mention that you could hand tie a quilt or hand stitch it as well as use a machine. Some women like to do hand quilting while they watch TV!

Using some of the string squares from the last guild meeting, she sewed four together, added batt, and machine quilted the top. Several of them expressed amazement that it was so easy with so few rules. She gave them some of the string squares and encouraged them to arrange them any way they wanted, then helped them stitch four together into pillow tops. By the end of the hour and a half, they all left with a project to finish and an invitation to stop by the guild meeting on Saturday for help or to become further involved in quilting.

One of them had introduced herself as Thelma Perkins and, after everyone else left, she confessed that she didn't have a sewing machine at home. Couldn't afford it.

Queenie gently told her she could sew by hand if she was comfortable with that. She explained that hand-sewn pieces were considered more authentic by some. The plain face lit up. "I can do that. I sew stuff all the time, you know, mending and all."

"Great. If you give me your number, I'll also check around and see if anyone has a machine they're not using."

"Don't have a cellphone." Thelma muttered. "But we do have a house phone." She wrote the number on a slip of paper and handed it to Queenie. "I sure do appreciate your help."

After a moment's hesitation, she pulled a small doll from her bag. "I been making these for some time now. I enjoy it."

Queenie was astonished. Thelma had embroidered a face that actually seemed to have an expression of joy and wonder onto a small stuffed muslin doll wearing a gingham dress. Rather than add yarn for hair she had actually embroidered a hairstyle onto the head. Queenie had honestly never seen anything like it.

"How on earth?"

A rare smile lit up Thelma's thin face. "I had one sort of like this when I was little, think my Grandma made it for me. It don't take more than some scraps."

Queenie closed her mouth which had fallen open. "Do you have more of these?"

"Oh sure."

She put an arm around the thin shoulders. "We need to talk."

Twenty Seven

Clark was startled out of a sound sleep by a pounding on his door. He awoke a bit disoriented as he had nodded off sitting in his favorite chair by the fire, his mystery slipping to the floor.

"Just a minute!" He couldn't imagine who would come calling at such an ungodly hour of...9:45!

He looked through the peephole to see a middle-aged man in a cheap suit.

"Yes?" He said impatiently.

"Clark Baxter?"

"Who are you and what do you want?"

"My name is Harry Logan. I represent a company interested in buying the land under the factory. Can I come in?"

Clark was furious. "No, you may not. Call my attorney in the morning! This is highly unacceptable!"

"Aw c'mon man. Just let me deliver this envelope so I can go the hell home!" He held up a manila envelope so Clark could see it.

Against his better judgment, Clark unlocked the door. It burst open and the last thing Clark saw was a huge fist coming at his wide eyes.

Gabe's phone rang at 5AM and, thanks to long years of practice, he was alert and upright in 10 seconds.

"Downing."

Miranda stirred a bit and Gabe lifted his robe off the hook silently and moved to the kitchen.

"Gabe."

"Jimmy?"

"Yeah. Sorry man. I hate to wake you but there has been an...incident."

"It's okay. Go on."

"It seems Clark Baxter attempted suicide last night."

Gabe hesitated. "Attempted?"

"Yes, he is alive, but barely, and unconscious."

"Where are you?"

"County Hospital."

"I'll be there in 10."

As Gabe pulled into the hospital lot, his cell beeped with a message from Miranda asking where he had gone so early.

"Crap."

He shot her a text apologizing for worrying her, saying Jimmy had called and he'd fill her in later. He got a red heart in return.

He walked through the lobby and saw Jimmy standing near the elevators. He looked exhausted as usual.

"Good morning Jimmy."

"Is it?"

Jimmy immediately regretted his flippant remark. He looked at Gabe and shook his head.

"I'm sorry."

Gabe laid his hand on Jimmy's shoulder.

"Tell me what happened."

Jimmy looked at his small notebook. "Apparently he had a breakfast meeting with Dennis. When he didn't show, Dennis went to his home. His car was there, lights were on. Dennis used his key and found Clark face down on the edge of the fireplace. He was alive but barely. Dennis called 911 and rode in with him.

"Breakfast at 6 am?"

"I know. Apparently the old man rallied the boys at 5 am every day but Sunday."

"The Lord's day of rest?"

"Exactly."

"So they got the day off?"

"No, they got to sleep until seven, then were off to church for four hours."

Gabe felt a sudden wave of sympathy for Dennis and Clark. "I'm not asking any more questions."

Jimmy smiled. "So it plays like an attempted suicide, but I don't like it."

"Suicide?? Why on earth?"

"Exactly. Plus it appears to be a combination of alcohol and sleeping pills. He tried to get up, fell forward and landed on his face on the fireplace stone."

Gabe thought about it. "That is suspicious. He just inherited four mill and men, in general..."

"Don't kill themselves with drugs."

Gabe was impressed. "Exactly, so let's go take a look." He called Miranda on his way to Clark's. As he started to explain, she interrupted. The Cutler grapevine had already been humming with the news. "Oh honey! Did he really try to kill himself?"

"I'm not sure and neither is Jimmy. We're on our way over there to look around."

"Keep me posted."

"You know I will."

Dennis sat next to Clark's bed. How on earth had it come to this? He had called Angela who said she would be back tomorrow; she had a manicure apt that afternoon. She didn't seem as shocked as he thought she would be. Of course she wasn't sentimental or affectionate, never had been. He started at the monitors and heard the soft beeps and whooshes. It seemed sort of silly, but he started making a deal with God.

Gabe pulled in behind Jimmy's squad car. As he had been on his first trip, Gabe was immediately drawn to the wood and the details carved in the massive front door.

"Beautiful," he murmured.

"What?" Jimmy turned to Gabe.

"The workmanship on this door is spectacular." He looked at Jimmy. "It's also heavy and well-made."

Jimmy picked up on Gabe's thought. "So if someone got in, it's because he let them in."

"Exactly."

Jimmy turned the key and they walked into Clark's home.

It was, as Gabe remembered, well-appointed in dark wood, deep jewel tones of green and red and blue, a large reading chair and brass lamp. The ashes in the fireplace had a faint smell of burnt wood. It was, in short, a man's room.

"Very cozy."

Gabe was momentarily lost in thought.

"What? oh yes, very warm."

"You know, being a long-time single, a bit soft, a little fussy..." Jimmy let the thought trail off

"This room seems too manly for Clark?" Gabe smiled.

Jimmy's face colored..."Yeah."

"I've heard the rumors, for now let's just see what's here, keep an open mind, and go where the evidence takes us."

Jimmy looked at Gabe. "Right as usual. Maybe you should take this job. I would be proud to be your assistant chief."

Gabe stared at him, then sputtered, "Miranda...kill...me."

Jimmy laughed as he started looking at Clark's mail.

Twenty Eight

He made it to the station about half an hour before the big mobile investigation unit pulled in. It was larger than an RV and slightly smaller than an 18-wheeler.

Two men and a woman got out of it and went straight inside the station and asked Trixie for the Chief. Jimmy came out to greet them and was surprised that they were dressed casually in jeans and jackets. The leader explained with a smile that they'd be donning white jumpsuits and shoe covers on scene.

He took them into the interrogation room. They cast eyes upon the old paint and worn furniture but said nothing. He offered them coffee and they declined.

"We're all set. Thanks."

He answered their questions and gave them a copy of Dick Dixon's report. Then he handed over the white quilt in its plastic covering.

"We should get started then."

As they turned to leave, Jimmy asked, "You'll be checking for fingerprints, right?"

Tim Ruskin, the leader of the group, nodded. Then he smiled. "Someone you have in mind, Chief?"

"Maybe."

"I figure we'll be done by end of day, if not sooner. We'll check back in before we leave."

Jimmy gave them his cell in case he was out of the office when they were finished.

He was impressed. He wished he could watch them work at the factory. But that would be unprofessional. He chuckled at himself. Nothing said local yokel like standing around watching the pros do their jobs.

The state investigators had finished up inside the factory by mid-afternoon. Then they went into their mobile unit and completed testing. The computer spit out the reports and they emailed the results to Jimmy.

They came into the office looking a bit weary but handed him a printed copy of their findings.

"Since you asked about prints specifically, we took prints from the office which will likely allow you to eliminate the owners. Of course, there were numerous prints on the line where the plant workers would have been and in their breakroom.

"There is one set that we found on the gas line that was clearer than the rest, meaning those prints were the most recent ones which is interesting considering the age and overall condition. The line itself was actually pierced in two places. These cuts were so small we only saw them when we used a microscope on the pieces that were left and by determining where the actual explosion took place using the spread pattern.

"As to the fabric piece, we can tell you with certainty that it was set on fire on one end. It was then tossed into the machinery on the far side from the gas line. The perp counted on it moving forward on fire until it hit the gas which they had caused to leak, albeit slowly.

In short, the perp cut the gas lines, went round the other side of the machinery, lit the fabric, and placed it on the cogs and saw it start moving forward. They undoubtedly ran off before the explosion. It would have taken maybe 6-8 minutes before it blew."

Jimmy could see the whole thing in his mind and he felt sick. "Our fire marshal said the fabric caught, slowed the machine, it sparked and set off the gas line." He swallowed. "He said there was no way the person could really have known what would happen."

The female investigator nodded. "That's what it might have looked like without our lab. He couldn't have seen that the gas line was nicked. He couldn't have examined the fibers of the fabric without a serious microscope." She shook her head sadly. "This was arson, chief, pure and simple."

At the look on his face, the other investigator added, "If it helps, in addition to those left on the gas line, there are fingerprints on that fabric that are probably clear enough to check against your suspect's."

He pulled out a report. "There were other prints on the fabric, of course, no doubt from when it was presented and hung. But this set is only on the end that was lit on fire and they're fresh, too clear to be very old."

Jimmy was embarrassed to find his hands shaking as he accepted the report and shook their hands. They smiled sympathetically, told him to contact them with any questions. They departed quick and silently, job done, knowing that they were leaving the young chief with the worst part of the job to do.

For Jimmy, it made for a sleepless night.

Twenty Nine

He wasn't the only one. She couldn't believe it. Angela was refusing to take her calls. That bitch. Marlo was exhausted and angry when the police car pulled up to her office.

This time, the DA sat with Jimmy as they showed her reports indicating that her fingerprints were on the white quilt.

"Is there anything you'd like to tell us about this?"

"I want a lawyer."

"Excellent idea." Said the DA. "Call him now."

"I don't actually know one," she said in a whisper.

Jimmy sighed. "The best, and frankly only, criminal attorney around here is Peter Knowles. Do you want his number?"

She nodded and he left the room and returned with a business card. They gave her the room for a few minutes.

No one was surprised that Peter said he could be there in half an hour. He loved the headlines and this was probably going to make news across the state, if not the nationals.

When they were finally settled, after Attorney Knowles had spent a few minutes with his client, the questioning began.

Once again, they explained that her fingerprints had been found on the white quilt.

She looked at her attorney. "I did see the quilt and I touched it."

"When?"

"After it was hung in the office."

"So you were in the office?"

"Yes."

"For what purpose?"

She trembled a bit. "I went there to try to convince Carl to sell. I needed that contract."

"Go on."

"He was on the floor of the factory and I had to wait. The quilt was pretty and I touched it."

"Where?"

"What?"

"Where did you touch it? Did you put your hand in the center? Or touch the edge? Where?"

She thought about it. "I don't remember."

The DA, Mike Church, looked at her attorney. "Your fingerprints were found at the edge of the quilt where it was set on fire."

Knowles spoke up. "Coincidence, surely."

Jimmy looked at Marlo who would not meet his eyes. He sighed and pulled out an enlarged photo.

"This is the gas line that was punctured before the explosion and that's your fingerprint." He pointed. "Is that a coincidence too? Are you simply fascinated by gas lines?"

"There's no need for sarcasm." Her attorney said.

"Then explain."

"No comment."

Jimmy softened his tone. "You are aware that a man died because of this."

The tears started to run down her face, leaving streaks in her make up.

Her attorney put a hand on hers. "Say nothing."

"Can I have some water?"

When it was provided, she took a deep drink.

Jimmy pulled out a recorder and played the tape for her that he had recorded earlier. "Something you should hear."

"Marlo Perkins? She's a realtor, right? I've met her, of course, but I can't say we're friends."

Marlo's eyes widened.

"Are you saying she blew up the factory? Ohmigod, she must have been desperate to get us to sell."

He clicked it off. "Enough?"

The woman seemed to shrink as she crumpled at the table.

"It was Angela." It came out as a whisper.

Her attorney spoke harshly. "Say nothing more, I beg you."

She shook him off. "No, I'm done being the villain." She sobbed. "Now she won't even take my calls."

They took a break while she composed herself with her attorney speaking urgently and Marlo shaking her head.

When they resumed, the DA spoke first. "Please be reminded that this conversation is being recorded."

Then he read her the Miranda rights that are required prior to an arrest. "You have the right to remain silent…"

"I understand." Now composed, she said her piece. "Angela Baxter and I were...partners. She was frustrated by her father and brothers not listening to any of her ideas to update the place and she was sick of the smell of chocolate. She came up with the idea to damage the plant. That's all it was meant to be."

She took a breath. "She called me and told me that she had ripped down that stupid quilt and maybe that was a way to make sure there was damage. We had been going to just puncture the gas line and light a cord some feet away but the fabric was better. It would certainly look like an accident and it seemed safer, like I'd have more time to get out. I went down there and saw Fred in his booth, fast asleep. So I did it. I cut two tiny holes in the line, lit the fabric and tossed it into the machine from the other side. Then I ran. Period."

She shuddered a little. "He was asleep, I swear to God. He should have been safe." Then she added bitterly, "I'm an idiot, okay? She promised me a new life away from this town and, instead, she played me."

Jimmy stood. "Marlo Perkins, you are under arrest for arson and involuntary manslaughter."

He should have been relieved but all he felt, as he and the DA conferred after locking her up, was sadness and a little sick.

"Is Angela going to get away with it?"

Mike shrugged. "If we can't find any proof beyond Marlo's testimony, she'll walk."

Jimmy thought about it. Then he called a friend.

Thirty

I should have known something was up when Harry followed me to the door as I was leaving for work, talking a blue streak. I picked him up and looked into his beautiful eyes.

"Is something happening, Harry?"

"Yeeooowwww."

"Is it a good thing?"

He explained in Catish and I gave him a moment. I knew better than to let him know I couldn't understand a word.

"Okay, so everything's going to be all right then?"

"Yeoooowww."

I kissed his little nose and went to work.

I was surprised by Jimmy's call, to say the least, and a bit nervous. But he had asked and I had no good reason to say "no" so I picked up lunch from Sylvia's and Trixie, the dispatcher/receptionist, made a show of examining it. We both smiled as she picked up the plastic knife and raised an eyebrow.

She unlocked the cell. Marlo sat curled up in the corner.

"Hungry?" I asked.

The woman sat up and nodded. I set the bag down on the edge of the cot and settled myself in the small plastic chair. I pulled out two sandwiches and a small container of soup for Marlo, handing her napkins and the plastic spoon. I had two bottles of iced coffee and two cookies.

We ate in silence. After she gulped down the food, Marlo turned suspicious eyes on me.

"What are you doing here? I already told them all I know."

I replied honestly, "I'm not sure. Jimmy asked me to see if I could help you so I came."

"Why?"

I shrugged. "Well, for one thing, I've always felt that the Perkins family got kind of a rough go from this town. Especially you kids."

Marlo nodded bitterly. "I'd have changed my name if I thought it would do any good."

"Understandable. But that doesn't give anyone the right to take advantage."

"You mean Angela."

"I mean anyone."

Marlo's eyes narrowed. "Are you wearing a wire?"

I choked on my cookie. "What?" Then I laughed out loud and Marlo even smiled. "Oh, like they do on TV. No, honey, I'm not. And I don't think this place has the money to wire the cells, do you?" I patted my chest and lifted the edge of my sweater.

Marlo raised a hand. "Okay, I believe you."

"Well, good, it would have been embarrassing for both of us if I'd had to strip."

Then she got the giggles and it was contagious until we were both wiping our eyes.

"Thanks, I needed that." Marlo gasped.

I stood, gathering the trash. "I have to get back to work." I laid a hand on Marlo's shoulder. "I am sorry that this has happened to you."

"Thanks." Marlo's head went down.

Later that afternoon, the intercom went off in Jimmy's office.

"She'd like to see you." Trixie's voice came through.

Jimmy took Gus with him as a witness when he walked back to Marlo who was calmer now.

She said, "I've decided I'm taking her down with me." She took a breath. "The phone. It's at my house." At their blank looks, she added impatiently, "The phone Angela called me that night, it's at my house in the desk."

"Presumably, she called you on a burner."

Marlo nodded. "Sure, but I taped the call. I don't know what I was thinking. Maybe I was finally getting the idea that she meant for me to be the patsy. It's not much but it's something." Then her face lit up. "Wait. There is also some money in the desk that she gave me. Her prints will be on it, right? I saw on TV where you can match it to money she withdrew from the bank or something."

Jimmy's mouth fell open.

"Your cooperation will be duly noted, Marlo."

"I sure as hell hope so." Then she took a breath. "Just promise me we'll go to different jails, okay?"

Thirty One

Dennis had his head resting on the edge of Clark's hospital bed. He felt a soft touch on his face and jumped.

"Hey!"

Clark smiled, then grimaced. "My face hurts."

Dennis smiled, "That's too easy…"

"Heh. I know, it's killing you."

They looked at each other.

"What happened?"

"You don't remember anything?"

Clark closed his eyes. "It's really fuzzy."

His brother nodded. "The doctors said that you might have some short-term memory loss but it should be temporary."

"Okay. Can you tell me what happened?"

Dennis hesitated. "Right now, I think we should get the nurse and let the doctor know you're awake. And get you some water and food. After the docs give you the okay, we can talk."

"All right. And Dennis? Thanks, bro."

Jimmy's desk phone rang. Gabe glanced up.

"Hello? Really? That is excellent news, let me know when we can come by. Right. Bye.

He met Gabe's eyes. "Clark Baxter is awake."

"Wow, is he…functioning normally?"

"Seems so, he is getting a full work-up but Dennis said they had a normal conversation."

Before Gabe could answer, the phone rang again.

"Damn," Jimmy muttered.

"Yes?

Gabe sat quietly as Jimmy listened intently.

"Yes, go ahead and roll on it, bring him in."

"There's a low-life lives in a trailer just outside of town, Barry Ripka, petty crimes, d and d, and just a loud-mouthed jerk. Apparently he's been flashing cash and buying big-ticket items. Told the barmaid at Toner's he did a job and hit it big. Joey is going out there to pick him up."

"Well now, isn't today becoming eventful?"

"And it's not over yet. Angela Baxter's on her way back."

To say that Angela Baxter was surprised when the NYPD showed up at her apartment would be an understatement. But when she started kicking and spitting at them, things got worse for her.

By the time they got her back to Cutler, she was bad mouthing everyone she could think of. When Jimmy had to tell her she was going to be sent to County because Cutler had only the two cells and they were full, she hit the roof.

She knew one of them would be Marlo and she insisted that Marlo be sent to County. Why should she have to go? Angela was more important. She would hire an attorney that would make Peter Knowles look like the local yokel he was and the DA only had the job because his dad had it before him.

Waiting for the county car to show up, they put her into the interrogation room and had to handcuff her to the table. That went over well.

Jimmy called Dennis and explained. He was there in ten minutes. He walked into the room and sat down next to his sister. He simply took her hand without speaking. Angela went quiet, then she laid her head on his shoulder and he put his other arm around her.

Sitting in the cell next to Marlo, Barry Ripka was thinking how this sucked. He finally gets a break and somebody rats him out.

Jimmy Haines unlocked the door and came in, sitting down next to him on the thin mattress.

"Barry. I heard you been passing some serious bucks all over town. What's goin' on?"

"I won the lottery."

Jimmy had to smile. "Try again."

"It's the truth!"

"Okay, you can stay here until I verify that. Where'd you buy the ticket?"

"Aw crap."

"And there's more. Clark Baxter is awake and his description of his attacker sounds remarkably like...you!"

"Nope. Wasn't me."

"Yep. And right now, Gus is on his way to the hospital with a photo line-up card. What do you think the odds are of Clark pickin' you out?" He stood. "Time's up, Ripka. Ready to tell me the whole story?

"Crap."

Jimmy took Barry to the interrogation room. He turned on the recorders and sat back.

Ripka cleared his throat. "Okay, So I'm sittin' at home drinking a beer and watchin' the Pirates. My phone rings and a voice says, 'Just listen close and don't talk.' So I listen. They tell me there's this guy who needs to be handled, and can I do it."

"Go on."

He drew a deep breath. "Tells me there's a brown bag in my cooler out front. Has everything I need and tells me how to do it. There's also 2500 bucks. I darned near tore a hammy running out there!"

Again, Jimmy resisted the urge to laugh. "Barry, you know this is attempted murder."

"Whaaaat? Oh heck no."

"Tell me exactly what you did at Clark's."

Barry sighed. "I don't like to fight, I'm not violent."

"Except with women." Jimmy shot back. "Go on."

Barry gave him a dirty look, then went on. "Whatever. They left me this envelope and said to tell him I had to give it to him. I got to the place, and he don't wanna open the door so I keep talkin'. He finally opened the door and I punched him in the face. He dropped like a lead balloon.

"In the bag was a water bottle. It smelled like gin. I picked up his head and poured it down his throat, then I sort of, uhm, turned him over and dropped him on the fireplace facedown."

Jimmy took a few seconds to choose his words

carefully.

"Barry, did you drink any of the gin?"

His face turned red. "I took a sip, it was awful."

"That's because it was laced with drugs."

"What are ya talkin' about?"

"You weren't there to scare him, you were sent there to kill him and make it look like he killed himself. What else did she tell you?"

"Nothing! I didn't have any idea—wait, she?"

"Wasn't the person who called you female?"

"Nooo. It was a man, actually sounded like an old dude, like really old."

Well now, Jimmy thought, doesn't that screw up his theory.

"Jesus."

Barry jumped to his feet. "You watch your mouth, boy. Momma don't hold with cursing, specially taking the Lord's name in vain."

Jimmy nodded and stifled. He made it as far as his office before collapsing into his chair.

Gus stuck his head in. "You all right there, Chief?"

Jimmy blurted out the story and Gus was wiping tears from his eyes when Trixie came over to see what was so funny. Within minutes, the story was making the rounds of the town.

When Gabe called in, Jimmy shared the story with him. There was silence.

"But isn't Momma…"

"Yep, 6'2", about 240 and not an ounce of fat, neither."

"And doesn't she run…"

Jimmy struggled to control himself. "Yep. She runs girls out of that big old farmhouse but we can't get anyone to file a complaint."

Truth was, she treated the girls like her own and most of them had better lives than they had at their own homes. A couple of them were out at the community college.

It was Gabe's turn to burst into laughter. "So you're saying she doesn't mind most things."

Mimicking Barry, Jim answered, "But Momma don't hold with cursing."

When he was able to catch his breath, Jimmy muttered, "I needed that."

Trixie stuck her head in, put a hand on her hip, and crooned, "If you're good to Momma,"

Chicago being one of his favorite musicals, Jim grinned and finished, "She'll be good to you."

Thirty Two

Clark sat straight up and stared at Dennis.

"SUICIDE? Are you insane? Why on earth would I do that? My life is wonderful! And I could never do that to you, or Ange, after we just lost Dad.

Dennis looked down at the floor. Just then Gabe and Jimmy walked into the room.

Gabe spoke, "Clark, you look much better than a few days ago."

There was a distinct chill in the room. Clark was clearly angry and Jimmy asked about it.

Clark looked at Dennis. "My brother was just explaining to me how my assault was first ruled an attempted suicide. Perhaps you'd care to explain, Sheriff?"

Jimmy cleared his throat. "Well Mr. Baxter, I know being an older, single man with fine tastes in a small town life can be hard on, uh, a sensitive guy like you."

Clark digested that for a moment. "Ohmigod. You all think that I'm gay?"

And then he started to laugh.

"Seriously, gay?"

Dennis looked ashamed. "Well you gotta admit, you are extremely neat, and you have never had a girlfriend, or even talked about one!"

"Because dear brother, I am a gentleman."

At that moment the door burst open and a very attractive, well-dressed woman with big green eyes ran to Clark's side and gently wrapped her arms around him. He kissed the top of her head.

"Allow me to introduce my partner in life, Teresa Fleisher."

Three stunned faces stared at the scene on the bed. Teresa lifted her head and managed a small nod. Clark got over his initial shock and realized that she had blown the cover of secrecy they guarded so closely.

"Teresa, what are you doing here? Your father…"

"Is a monster. He did this, Clark, he did this to you and to me!"

"Honey, calm down and tell me what you mean."

Gabe added, "Yes please."

"Okay. Clark and I met many years ago at a matinee of 'Singin' in the Rain'." They looked at each and smiled and the love in their faces was unmistakable.

"We began dating; meeting for coffee, going to dinner, plays, taking long walks, falling in love. I introduced him to my parents. I thought they would see that he is perfect for me. Then my father asked him what church he attended."

Her gaze dropped and Clark reached to hold her hand. "I come from a very strict Catholic family complete with priests and fish on Fridays. When my Father found out Clark wasn't Catholic, he was livid. He forbade me to ever see him again. I cried for two weeks. I begged, I lashed out, I stopped eating. Then he started bringing good Catholic men from church home for dinner. Irish guys, Italian guys, but my heart was like stone. I was in love with Clark so deeply, instead of fading, the separation only made it stronger."

He looked at her with misty eyes. "As did mine."

She kissed him ever so gently.

"So we started seeing each other secretly. I know it sounds ridiculous at this age but my father is very powerful and frankly, he scares me."

"Apparently for good reason," Jimmy said.

Teresa nodded. "He told me it would be over his dead body I'd marry a non-Catholic man. He had me followed. He's been becoming more and more unreasonable and somewhat volatile." She took a breath. "This morning, he told me that Clark was dead."

She shook her head. "I admit I screamed at him until I couldn't, anymore.

"Then he suddenly turned purple and grabbed his head with both hands. My mother called 911. It's a stroke. He's in a coma." She turned back to Clark. "My mother told me what he did. I knew you wouldn't harm yourself."

Tears ran down her cheeks. "You would never do that to me."

He squeezed her hand. "Never."

Thirty Three

The whole town knew it was coming. But when the bulldozers and dump trucks started pulling down what was left of the front of the factory, the townspeople were stunned.

There had been no news, no announcements. Paychecks kept coming, insurance was paid, and pensions were honored. The folks in Cutler had enjoyed the respite and had stopped fretting about how long it would last.

Now, there was demolition and Dennis Baxter and Professor Joseph Martin from Penn State were on site, talking and walking around. What did that mean?

When they walked into the Mayor's office and the inner office door closed behind them, the buzz escalated all over town.

To the great relief of all, a town meeting was called for the following evening. The town hall was packed.

Dennis stood and the crowd quieted. "I know what a hard time this has been for all of you. I'm sorry there has been so little information. Chief Haynes has done an amazing job determining the cause of the fire. He has authorized me to tell you that, based on the report of the state investigators and his own interviews, Marlo Perkins has been arrested for arson and involuntary manslaughter."

A gasp rose from the crowd followed by murmurs and he raised his hand for quiet.

Then he added in a pained voice, "And Angela Baxter is being indicted on charges of accomplice to those crimes."

A slow roar of indignation and anger rose. He gave them a moment, then went on.

"That may give us some closure, especially for Fred, but it doesn't help us save the jobs that are currently on hold. As you have seen, we have started to tear down the damaged part of the factory." He swallowed hard and sighed. "I have the duty to announce to you that the candy factory will not be re-opening—not as it was."

The crowd quieted.

"With the help of the mayor and Professor Martin from Penn State, we've created a plan to turn the factory into a bottling plant."

As they sat there stunned, he unveiled a logo. "Ladies and gentlemen, I give you Sunny Springs water. The container will be recyclable material and the plant will be green and environmentally sustainable. As you may imagine, we will be completing paperwork as fast as we can to get this moving."

The stunned crowd stared.

One of the men stood. "But what about our jobs?"

Dennis nodded. "I hear you, Pete. Everyone who worked at the candy factory will be retrained to work at Sunny Springs if they want to. We will be holding meetings and sessions in the high school auditorium within the next few weeks. I encourage you to give it a chance. You can do this;

we can do this. I will personally make sure you have a job. If you don't like working there, we will place you somewhere else. We will continue to pay your salary and insurance until you have secured a new position." He added with a grin, "I am hoping that we all find water easier to work with than chocolate."

The man started to applaud and soon the hall was rocking with approval.

Once they settled, he spoke again.

"How are we doing this, you might ask. So here's the plan for now. You all know that the insurance company is not going to pay for the damage to the building.

"The Country Candies Company is buying several recipes for our best selling items. That will go a long way to the retrofit.

"The state Small Business Bureau is standing by to help. Sandy Tressler, our mayor, has been front and center finding some federal grants for us as an environmentally progressive plant. This is a cooperative effort." He took a breath. "While the plant is being refitted in the damaged area, we are going to go back to making candy until we've used up as much of our inventory as we can. Anyone who wants to be involved in that should show up to the plant Monday morning at 8 o'clock."

The meeting broke up with handshakes and more questions about the new jobs aimed at Dennis and Sandy. But the veil of uncertainty and fear lifted.

Dennis didn't mention his private meeting with Melody Hutchins and with Jimmy Haynes. Once they had access to

Angela's bank records, it was pretty easy to prove that she had paid Fred the $10,000 to damage the plant. It was likely that Fred's role would come out in the upcoming trials. Maybe it wouldn't. But Jimmy did his job and asked Melody to return the funds to his office.

At the same time, Dennis presented Melody with a check for $100,000, explaining that, although as a part-time employee, Fred hadn't accumulated a pension, it had been his intent all along to reward Fred a pension for long service. Melody was moved beyond words, that is, she literally couldn't seem to speak but took the check with shaking hands.

Thirty Four

The phone rang early Sunday morning and I put down the paper. Zoey. My heart took a leap.

"Calm down, Mom. I'm okay."

"Whew. Good." Then I added without thinking, "Lord, I'll be glad when this is over."

She replied at once, "YOU????"

"Sorry."

"Okay, I called to tell you we closed on the house yesterday and we're moving. We're pulling all the pieces together. If you and Gabe could come up on Saturday, that would be great. Kevin and Terry are coming over. The house is in Newton and they're just a few blocks away."

"We'll be there, honey. So exciting. Now…"

"Yes, Mom. We are having movers pack and stay to help place furniture. All I have to do is point."

"That'll work. And I'll be there to be sure you do."

"Mom? Do you think you could get, like a whole meatloaf from Sylvia's? I am so craving her meatloaf."

"Absolutely."

"Okay. Lots to do. Bye!"

I stood there holding the phone. What did she mean, lots to do? She wasn't supposed to be doing anything! I resisted the urge to call back.

I texted Dee to let her know the latest, that we'd be heading to Massachusetts. I could work out an extra day or two off with Lucy tomorrow.

Gabe and Harry and I were catching up on our Jeopardy later when the phone rang. Having completed her usual Sunday duties (church, then dinner with the in-laws), Dee wanted to hear about Zoey. We chatted for a few minutes, then Gabe signaled for the phone.

"It's Dee," I whispered.

"I know."

I handed him the phone tentatively.

"Hey Dee, may I ask you something?"

"Sure, I am happily married but I could be reasonable if it was worth my while."

Gabe choked. "Okay then. I've been wondering about Clark Baxter and Teresa Fleisher." He thought it best to give a little. "The DA isn't filing charges against the old man until or unless he comes out of the coma." He paused. "But I was wondering if everybody knew…"

She laughed. "Oh, the anonymous "friend" thing? It is pretty weird."

"Yes. It's none of my business, of course."

"Nor mine. But I can tell you, most of us knew. Clark has been seeing Teresa for, oh, I'd say five years now easy. You know about the RC thing.

"One interesting tidbit is that her mother knew the whole time. She didn't really mind like the father did. She realized Clark was a good guy.

"Another fun fact is that apparently David Fleisher's religious beliefs don't extend to his import-export business. He really is a dangerous guy to make an enemy of. He's been bringing in truckloads of prescription drugs from Canada for a couple of years now and selling them all over the state.

"So it was Mary, her mother who convinced David to put the house on the market and join their relatives in Florida. She and Teresa were telling him what he wanted to hear, that Teresa would be fine on her own and stuff.

"But, of course, as you know, the old guy found out and decided getting rid of Clark was the way to go."

"Dear Lord, how do you know all this?"

"Oh please." She lowered her voice. "I could tell you but…"

Gabe laughed so hard he had to hand the phone to Miranda.

Thirty Five

After the trials were over, Dennis Baxter made a trip to Queenie's Quilt Shop. He handed her the bag with the moldy mess.

"I'd like to have this back. Do you think you can do it?"

She took a breath. "I can try." She paused. "Cutler Quilt Guild #1 will do its best for you. We know you've done your best for us."

He nodded, swallowing hard. "Thanks."

He turned to the door, then turned back with a grin. "This time, I think we'll hang it in the Town Hall."

She smiled back. "Good idea."

AUTHOR'S NOTE:

We have become aware that the R.M. Palmer Candy Factory in West Redding Pennsylvania was damaged by an explosion on Saturday, March 25, 2023. In that terrible accident, seven people lost their lives and ten were injured. Please know that we began to write this book approximately six months before that explosion. Any similarities are purely coincidental. Our hearts go out to all of those affected by this tragedy.

Meet the authors...

Mary Devlin Lynch lives in the Bronx but spends a few winter months in Florida. She's a notorious multitasker, often working on several quilts at a time, writing two books at the same time, and reading at least one book a week. She also handles the paperwork for her doctor husband's practice, loves tag sales, enjoys a trip to the casino (esp. with her sister), and handles the administrative side of devlinsbooks. Her daughter, Megan, son-in-law Peter, and grandsons, Collin and Luke, live in Natick, Massachusetts.

Beth Devlin-Keune, the youngest Devlin sister, lives in Pennsylvania near her alma mater, Penn State, with two kittens, Maggie and Maddox. Her Administration of Justice degree and law enforcement experience gives her special insight into many of our characters. In addition to rooting on the blue and white, she is also a voracious reader, enjoys a trip to the casino, likes a fine single malt, and watches sports and true crime TV.

The Quilt Ripper, Book 1
The Missing Quilter, Book 2
The Quilt Show Caper, Book 3
The Quilter's Secret, Book 4
A Quilt to Die For, Book 5
The Quilter's Christmas Surprises, Book 6
The Quilters Push Back, Book 7
The Quilting Queen, Book 8
The Quilting Cruise, Book 9
The Baby Quilt, Book 10
The Dollhouse Quilt, Book 11

Darcy Garrett Art Shop Mystery
Stormscapes
Darcy's Snowscapes
Irelandscapes

A Fine Mess and A Wedding Dress

Kelly's Teapot Christmas
A Temptation Teapot Society Cozy Mystery

Made in the USA
Middletown, DE
24 August 2023